W9-BIV-616

12/2021

Substantial Justice

Substantial Justice

Daniel Ben-Horin

a novel

rare bird
los angeles, calif.

THIS IS A GENUINE RARE BIRD BOOK

Rare Bird/Vireo
453 South Spring Street, Suite 302
Los Angeles, CA 90013
rarebirdbooks.com

FIRST HARDCOVER EDITION

For more information, address:
Rare Bird Books Subsidiary Rights Department
453 South Spring Street, Suite 302
Los Angeles, CA 90013

Printed in the United States

10 9 8 7 6 5 4 3 2 1

Library of Congress Cataloging-in-Publication Data

Names: Ben-Horin, Daniel, author.
Title: Substantial Justice / Daniel Ben-Horin.
Description: Los Angeles, CA : Rare Bird Books, [2020]
Identifiers: LCCN 2020013028 | ISBN 9781644281123 (hardback)
Subjects: GSAFD: Mystery fiction.
Classification: LCC PS3602.E4645 S83 2020 | DDC 813/.6—dc23

LC record available at https://lccn.loc.gov/2020013028

Prologue

Ukiah, California, June 14, 1985

On the pitted forest road near Ukiah, Spider entertained Siobhan with an ode to the Citroën DS's self-leveling suspension, which could be manually set to a jaw-dropping fourteen inches. After a wet winter and a damp spring, Spider was maneuvering around a Chevy Suburban that had been abandoned in a deceptively deep mud puddle. "I bet that Chevy had eight inches clearance max," he said. "Off-road vehicle, my ass."

"You really rabbit on sometimes," Siobhan said.

"What I really need to emphasize," Spider said, "is that the DS clearance is true clearance because it's front wheel drive, so no low-hanging transaxle. Compare that with a Jeep or anything short of maybe a tank, and you will be astonished. I can't emphasize that too much." He grinned at her, and she stuck out her tongue. She looked to him like she hadn't aged a day since he'd gotten lucky with her ten years before, dancing to the Dusty Chaps in a Phoenix bar. She was the funny, lithe girl he'd always wanted to find, and so, on that distant April Fool's Day, he'd allowed himself to fall blithely, idiotically in love. It lasted two months. She moved to New York, became a lawyer. He hadn't seen her again until two days ago.

She'd worn her hair long in 1975. Now, she'd cut it all off, leaving just a sophisticated coating of red fuzz, a fawn's coat, slightly thicker on top. It took some getting used to, but Spider was happy to put in the time.

Spider's hair had been long back then too, and it still was: kempt enough, straight and dark, descending below his shoulders. He felt a little stuck in time. His beard was still whimsically cut, with little effort at symmetry, as it had been since he returned from Vietnam in 1970. He hadn't wanted anyone to think he was just this or just that—just an oversized hippie, or just a Viet vet, or just an auto mechanic. He wanted to give folks a little "Huh?" when they took him in. He was slightly gap-toothed, which made him look simpler than he was.

Last Monday in San Francisco, Spider had been on his back with his arms deep inside a Citroën's underbelly when Mikael, his Volvo guy, said there was a call for him. Spider rolled out on his dolly to take the handset and felt his stomach knot when he heard her voice.

"Spider," she said. "It's Siobhan. I'm riding out your way to rescue the gyppos."

These were nonunionized loggers, she explained. Someone had been dumping poison on them. Might be class action material. He heard the words, but all he could think about was seeing her again.

She flew out on Friday; they spent most of Saturday in bed. He'd been nervous about that. Her new haircut and stylish clothes made him fear she had a matching array of obnoxious new bedroom tricks. But if she knew new tricks, she was wise enough not to parade them. For him, she was the best ever. Always had been.

Now it was Sunday evening and they were in Mendocino County, two hours and change north of San Francisco. She needed to interview gyppos who logged in the surrounding forest. They would stay with Spider's friend, Yosh, who lived—very well on his pot earnings—about four miles outside Ukiah.

•••

AFTER SIOBHAN'S 1975 DEPARTURE, ARIZONA RAN DRY FOR Spider and he moved to the coast. He'd been in San Francisco less than a month when a gruff fireplug of a guy named Yosh emerged from behind a refrigerator at a Bernal Heights party and convinced Spider that a property up for sale off Cortland Street was perfect for a mechanic with a little capital to invest. Several hours and some very strong pot birthed The New People's Garage.

Yosh said you could parse it as a garage for a new kind of people, or as a new garage for the people. "Plus, it has a kind of racy New People's Army sound to it, like you're in the Philippines or Nigeria or someplace like that."

The next year, Yosh decamped to two south-facing, state-forest-adjoining acres in the hills outside Ukiah. He grew weed in the forest. Of course he did. The timing was propitious. Sinsemilla, a new potent, seed-free strain, was wowing American potheads. It made people very high, without the downside of paralysis, which was the supposed result of smoking the Mexican pot that the US government was busily spraying with paraquat.

Yosh laundered much of his profit through a fresh vegetable business, utilizing a van festooned with BETTER LIVIN' THROUGH VEGETABLES and Mr. Natural cartoon figures. His personal experience with the Free Speech Movement, Weatherman, Panthers, and overall zeitgeist of the era had left him suspicious of just about everything. He presented his perspective in a vituperative and often comical fashion on a talk show he hosted on local public radio.

•••

THE SUN SET AS SPIDER NAVIGATED THE CITROËN along the forest road, Siobhan talked about her case. Class actions were tricky, she said. The law was highly specific. It was high-stakes legal poker.

"Gyppos," Spider said. "Nice ring to it. Was scumbags taken?"

"It's from the Greek, *gypas*, meaning vulture," Siobhan said. "Unattractive, but legally immaterial. Think of them as little Paul Bunyans with chainsaws," she said. "Doing the logging that union crews charge too much to do."

"So, union busters?"

"They're not precisely paragons of class struggle," Siobhan agreed. "In fact, everyone hates them. The lumber unions of course, and the environmentalists too. They're cheap labor, so the timber companies and mills exploit them." The topper, Siobhan said, was that their main employer, Bill Ricci's Redwood Pacific Lumber, had taken to casually bombing the gyppos with a defoliant called Garlon while they worked. "Agent Orange with lipstick," she said. "Why are you stopping here?"

Spider had hit the brakes at the top of a driveway that led to a white frame house. He nodded his head toward the house's front door, which was wide open. Something was sprawled across the welcome mat. Spider turned on his brights and drove slowly forward until they could see that it was a bloody mass the size of a man's body. "Fuck," Spider said. The head was visible now, and he could make out the frizzy gray hair that Yosh grew out of each side of his scalp, in homage, he said, to Larry of the Three Stooges. Two crows hopped in an anticipatory way next to the body. Spider could see that Yosh had been dead for a while, killed either by an army or an automatic weapon. He abruptly reversed back down the road, heeding long-buried instincts.

"We don't know who's out there," he said to Siobhan. "And there's nothing we can do for him."

It had been a long time between violent deaths for Spider. Since 1969, at a place the Vietnamese called Dong Ap Bia and the Americans called Hamburger Hill, where he saw his two best friends die within minutes of each other. Spider had then spent two hours inviting his own death, crisscrossing the field under heavy fire, saving a dozen lives and earning a Combat Medic Service Badge, the highest honor for his branch of duty. Death went missing from his life after Vietnam, and he liked it that way.

At the gas station, Siobhan got out with him and they embraced. Then he disengaged and called the sheriff's department.

Part I: Premortem

Chapter 1

Phoenix and San Francisco, 1975–1983

IT WAS A HOT APRIL NIGHT IN PHOENIX, with six more meltdown summer months yet to come. Spider, enervated from repairing cars all day, threw back two cold Dos Equis, smoked a joint, and listened once again to "Tangled Up in Blue." Finally, he mustered the energy to shower, change clothes, and prepare to do battle at Buffalo Benny.

Spider could get lucky there sometimes. Was he a hunky hippie or a hairy shitkicker? Some girls wanted to find out. And while in the outside world rock and roll was here to stay, at Buffalo Benny, western swing—a highly stylized permutation of polka, gypsy, Cajun, jitterbug, and square dancing—still ruled. Spider was proficient in the genre.

Some nights, slow nights when there weren't enough girls to go around, the cowboys and the freaks would turn their querulous attentions upon each other, and Spider might end up in a parking lot scrum. He had to admit he enjoyed these little macho interludes. He could take care of himself; that was something he'd brought home from Nam, along with the spiderweb of fine scars that crisscrossed his stomach, back, and legs. The army doctors had taken four slugs and sixty-seven pieces of shrapnel out of him after Hamburger Hill.

The evening's headliner, Clem Cline, had been big in Nashville, but not lately. A blowup of his current album cover dominated the bar's front window. The photo presented a comatose Clem amidst a sea of broken glass and overturned chairs and tables, in his hand a Bud longneck, its bottom severed.

Spider bought a beer and scoped the crowd. At a table near the dance floor, a man and woman were arguing, the woman jabbing with her finger as she raved, the man impassive, his eyes almost closed. The woman slammed down her glass and swept off into the crowd. The sound of the glass hitting the table seemed to arouse the man, who lurched forward as if to follow her. His legs, however, remained anchored. He threw a supplicating leer at the woman's back as he fell forward, his forehead thudding on the table, his Stetson toppling off to one side.

A redhead in the corner was observing the drama, too, and her eye caught Spider's. They both grinned, and Spider embarked on a great circle route to her table.

"Ladies," the lead singer of the warm-up band said, "I realize a lot of you feel thisaway about me the next morning, so don't think I'm a pig or nothing," and launched into the band's anthem, "(She Was Only) A Drunken Mistake."

"Dance?" Spider said.

When the redhead stood, it took her a while to uncoil. She was his height, six three, in her cowboy boots.

The homeliest woman can look like a queen
If you're drunk and you don't hesitate…

"That happen to you a lot? I'm Siobhan," she said as they two-stepped, each getting the feel of a new partner.

"Not even once," he said. "Spider is what I'm called."

He launched her into a spin before she could reply. Her height made the passes much easier, and she knew them all. Her rhythm was perfect, or at least the same as his. Spider initiated a complex sequence of moves off a back-pass culminating in a corkscrew. They slowed it down, nothing to prove, comfortable.

"You don't get drunk?" she said. "Or pick up homely women? Or don't care if you do? You're quite a large spider."

"The one in the middle," he said. "It beats Jeremiah. As a child, I was smaller."

The Dusty Chaps hustled off, and Clem Cline started to set up. Spider and Siobhan stayed put.

"What do you do?" she said. "Don't tell me." She held him at arms' length and looked him over. "You advise demented Czarina love slaves and instigate the overthrow of empires. You are Rasputin."

"I wish," Spider said. He had no idea who Rasputin was, but it sounded like he had an interesting gig. "What I do is work on cars."

"Outside my house," he added, and felt foolish for doing so.

Clem Cline glided into his big hit ballad of yesteryear, "Tell the Truth (Even If It Hurts)," a lugubrious account of his heedless penchant for intoxicants. They danced through the entire set in pleasant silence. When Clem subsided, they stood there. Spider didn't release her hand, and she didn't withdraw it.

"I don't suppose," she said, "that you work on Fiats?"

"You don't have to dance with me all night to get a service appointment," Spider said. She cackled. It was like something that would come out of the Wicked Witch. Spider fell in love.

Siobhan's Fiat was a needy vehicle from one of the Italian carmaker's vintage years when its workforce protested labor conditions by sabotaging the cars they were building. After Siobhan finished her workday as a probation officer, Spider would wheel himself under the jacked-up little car while she sat in an armchair with a beer and thumbed through the *Arizona Republic,* expostulating about events in the world. She'd toss a salad while he showered, and then they'd fuck all night.

She had a thing about Phoenix. Everyone did. It was a city you loved to hate in a state that had been the butt of the nation's jokes ever since the Barry Goldwater candidacy. She would find little tidbits in the *Republic* and yell them out to him while she was sitting on the can after sex.

"Only in Phoenix is there a citizens' petition to permit the shooting of feral cats on city streets."

"You gotta be a helluva shot to hit a moving cat," Spider said, lying in bed smoking a number, feeling like Phoenix wasn't actually as bad as all that.

Not that he intended to stay in Phoenix forever. But life was soft. Mexican bricks slid across the border. Psychedelics were the stuff of life—psilocybin for the most part, peyote for those who liked to throw up in a spiritually evocative fashion, acid of course, and mescaline for special occasions. You could jump in your car after work and make camp by ten in Aravaipa Canyon, high desert country, the canyon walls carved and painted by eons of wind and water. In the morning, you could drop shrooms, hike upstream in sneakers, and watch bats, canyon wrens, an occasional eagle, and the bighorn sheep on the ledges above. Spider and Siobhan spent one perfect weekend in Aravaipa, and then another that was better.

Spider's bungalow cost him ninety dollars a month. He had all the work he wanted. He played basketball twice a week, poker every Friday night, and softball on Sundays. And now, he had found Siobhan. She was the one, finally, with whom things were easy.

DANIEL BEN-HORIN

"I can't stay here, Spider," she said out of the blue, two months in. "I'll rot. We'll rot." She was going to New York to go to law school.

She didn't ask him to join her. He didn't ask to join. He was no New Yorker. He'd be an extra in her movie.

"We'll stay connected," she said. "Funny things happen. We're only twenty-five. I don't think I'm done with you, kiddo."

He stoically returned her goodbye embrace at the airport, then decided to drive up Camelback Mountain. When he was growing up, he had left the burgeoning town of Phoenix behind as he ascended the slope. The mountain roads were dirt then. But Camelback had become a checkerboard of paved roads leading to oversized grottos. The roads had names now—Wonderview, Grandview, Heavenly Vista, Panorama, Aerie Way, and Airy Lane—lest you miss the point.

The mountain looked awful this late afternoon. There were tendrils of plastic stuck to most of the saguaros, residue from the storm the week before. Shuffling, orange-bloused convicts dotted the landscape, purging the cacti of the detritus. The ostentatious mansions seemed to mock the mountain beneath them.

She was right, Spider could see that. Intelligent life wasn't supported by this ecosystem. Where, then? People he knew had gone to Boise, to Missoula, to Portland, and, of course, to San Francisco, which felt the scariest, a much faster place.

The evening wind was coming in now, hot out of the desert to the east. His eye seized upon a jumbo, bright red grocery bag, whipped by the breeze into a rigid perpendicularity, pointing toward the coast.

•••

IT WAS HARD TO THINK OF A REASON not to leave. There had been only one Siobhan in Phoenix; the chances of another blooming in that arid landscape seemed remote.

Spider called the softball pal who had moved to the Haight and urged him to visit. "No problemo," the guy said; there was a spare bedroom in his pad that Spider could rent. The guy forgot to mention the twin defecating schnauzers that belonged to the girl from Indiana who was in town for an indefinite period, squatting in the living room. He didn't mention the fleas either, which Spider contemplated on his ankles the first night in the new digs.

He picked his way through the turds to the living room, where the Hoosier girl was doing something to her toenails. "I have these things on my ankles," he informed her.

"California jumping fleas," she replied. "They only bother some people." She extended her comely calf toward him so he could confirm that she was not one of those beset. Her nails were tiny Cuban flags.

She smiled at him, rolled over attractively, and opened a drawer from which she extracted repellent and unguent. "Wear socks," she said.

The street outside was full of music and hair and the sweet smell of patchouli and cannabis. Siobhan really had been right, he thought. Phoenix was for rotting. San Francisco was for living. There were probably a million Siobhans out here.

He looked for the right opportunity to fix cars again. He had some money, almost twenty thousand, saved from five years working for twenty dollars an hour in front of his bungalow—cash only, paying no shop rent, keeping no books, paying no taxes. He could afford to wait a while, find the right situation.

It was slow going. San Francisco people were friendly enough, but there was a patronizing way they smiled when they heard where he was from that got on his nerves. It was a relief to find the Saturday morning full-court pickup basketball game at the Clipper Street playground, nice to just get sweaty and hoop.

Spider drove around an even bigger man under the basket and scooped in a reverse layup. "Barry to the rim," crowed one of his teammates, a little guy with a Groucho Marx mustache. It was a fun compliment—"Barry" being Rick, the god of basketball.

"Ben Ohanian," the guy said, drinking water after on the sidelines. "I like your game. You from the City?"

"Sort of," Spider said. "Phoenix."

"Well, you play a New York game," Ohanian said. "It must have been weird for you there." They exchanged further pleasantries and then Ohanian said, "You busy tonight? There's a good party in Bernal. Lots of local talent. They'll take to you like flies to shit."

But no flies tried to alight on Spider as he wandered the three floors of the shambly Victorian. No one even bothered to make eye contact. Finally, he worked up his courage and asked a skinny girl if she wanted to dance. She took her time acknowledging that he had spoken and then said, "No, but go ahead."

Spider felt wrong-footed. Arizona girls usually just stood up and started dancing. The party music was Motown, the tracks of Smokey's tears. He bowed gravely, said, "Thank you, ma'am," and turned toward the kitchen with as much dignity as he could muster.

A voice on the other side of the refrigerator rose above the hubbub. The voice was haranguing someone, making the point that decent left-wing radicals were being given a bad name in Middle America by the Symbionese Liberation Army and Patty Hearst.

"People out there aren't as stupid as all that," Spider said over the top of the refrigerator.

A short, swarthy fellow wheeled around the fridge to confront him. "The morons who elected Milhouse?" Then he turned less snappish. "A new face," he said. "Do you bring tidings from the hinterland?"

Tidings? It boiled down to what he had just said. People weren't any smarter in San Francisco. There was just more urgency here. Like this party! The crowd was determined to both rattle the cages of power and get laid before the sun rose. It was a tall order and it demanded determination, self-absorption, and drugs.

The swarthy man proffered a joint. "Give me your professional opinion," he said.

Spider took a short toke. The pot had actual flavor, not just hot smoke. He hadn't tasted anything quite like it. A rush went to his head.

His new friend viewed Spider's cautious pot intake with amusement. "A judicious man," he said. "But not, I think, a lawyer."

"I'm a mechanic," Spider said, once he realized he wasn't going to cough. "Or was one in Phoenix." He accepted a second hit. "Foreign cars. Cit…" Then he coughed, almost doubling over. It was very strong pot. "Citroëns a specialty, as I was saying," Spider said. "Now I got to set up shop here."

"A mechanic, no shit!" the man said. "I'm Yosh," he added. Spider introduced himself. He was wary of enthusiasm about his profession—it usually meant the other person wanted you to step outside and take a look at his oil leak. "I think this could be a significant interaction," Yosh said. "Let's talk a little more."

The skinny girl came into the kitchen. "I'm ready to dance now," she said to Spider, striking an engaging akimbo pose, twiddling her long straight hair. But Yosh intrigued him. He said, "Later, I hope," to the girl and followed Yosh out to the porch, with its view east toward the Bay, and then down the steps to the yard.

"Pretty good stuff, huh?" Yosh said. "Afghani seeds. Grown indoors." It was a different strain entirely from the Mexican pot Spider was used to. "Keep moving when you smoke this," Yosh said, "or you'll wake up where you sit down. I grow this in one room and mushrooms in the other. My apartment smells like the Amazon.

"Cut to the chase, I checked out this weird space just off Cortland today," he said. "Two flats over a warehouse. I said to myself, what a motherfucker of a garage this could be. It made me want to *become* a fucking mechanic, live upstairs, roll out of bed to work."

"You do this why?" Spider said. "Look at weird spaces? Like a hobby?"

Yosh laughed. "It's not about real estate," he said. "It's about bastions. What do you think is going to happen in this country?"

Everyone knew that stagflation, whatever that was, had the country by the balls. Oil prices were through the roof. You had to pay fifty cents a gallon to fill your car. Unemployment was out of control. On the other hand, Nixon had been forced to resign, and it looked like the Democrats had a good shot at the White House. "I really don't know," Spider said. "Do you?"

The directness of Spider's question seemed to take Yosh by surprise. "I think we have to dig in," he said. "Find safe places we can defend—economically, I mean. Businesses that can employ people. Land that can support people. So, yeah, it's my hobby now. My dad just shuffled off, and little Yoshie gets to play capitalist."

Yosh told Spider that he had already bought land outside Ukiah in Mendocino County. "The New People's Garage," he said, "is four blocks from here on Cortland." Spider realized he was speaking in the future tense. "I looked at the disclosures, and it needs a little work, but the foundation's solid, the roof's good, the plumbing works. A hundred thousand dollars. Think of the possibilities."

"I'm in for fifteen," Spider said.

"You're stoned," Yosh said.

"That's true," Spider said. "It's how I make decisions. I'm in."

They talked for a joint and half. Yosh offered to loan Spider an additional fifteen thousand, interest free, to make the down and improvements, and offered to cosign on the loan. Hell yeah, Spider thought. "Hell yeah," he said. "You're even crazier than I am."

•••

YOUNG PEOPLE HAD STARTED TO INFEST THE BERNAL Hill neighborhood right at the sixties' end, borrowing from their parents to buy and semi-restore big rundown houses on untended five-thousand-foot lots.

On the north side of the neighborhood, the hill itself, five acres of sedimentary silicate rock pushed up eons ago, full of iron oxide, shale and jasper, glittered in the afternoon sun. Dogs ran free on the Hill, as did drug consumption. Spider felt at home. The New People's Garage went house afire from the get-go.

Spider ate breakfast and took his work breaks at Belle's Café around the corner. You could soak up correct politics by osmosis at Belle's. When the building was bought by a speculator who tried to flip it, locals organized the "Dump Belle? Like Hell!" movement and promised an eternal boycott of any business that moved into the space. When the press came around, the locals pushed to the forefront as spokesperson a solid citizen—robust and bearded with a friendly gap tooth, a decorated Vietnam vet, a landlord himself, renting out one of the flats that adjoined his trendy New People's Garage. Spider ticked the media's boxes. By the time it was over, he was a small-scale public figure.

Romantically, San Francisco proved a good place to be Spider. He came to understand that he was an exotic, a man who actually worked with his hands. Most of the men he ran into talked about or wrote about such fellows, or acted them, or painted them. It was a cerebral, artistic, political environment, with which Spider contrasted easily.

Maybe too easily. Relationships abounded but got so far and no further.

Sometimes, when a romance went pear-shaped, Spider called Siobhan. He didn't quite know why. It was pathetic, and he had vowed on several occasions to never do it again.

"Who'd you break up with this time?" Siobhan had said the last time he called her.

"An extremely principled person. Gave me the boot."

Siobhan laughed. "I'm sorry," she said, "I shouldn't laugh. Did you love her?"

"No," Spider said. "Didn't get to that stage."

"She probably figured that out."

"Maybe," Spider said. "Her stated reason was my lack of political consciousness."

"Have you grown a political consciousness?"

"A little one," he said. "Not big enough, I guess. Size matters."

They agreed it was probably for the best. The conversation stalled.

"How's the class action biz?" Spider said.

"Oh, it's good," she said. "We're on a winning streak."

"Do you actually collect?"

"It can be stalled forever, but usually, yes," she said. "Most of the time. Sometimes."

"Pretty much never?"

"No!" she said, laughing. "I didn't say that."

He still made her laugh. Her cackle still got to him.

Ending calls with Siobhan was always challenging. "Well," Spider said. "Until the next time I get the shaft."

"Yeah," she said. "I can't wait."

It was just a quick, New York thing to say. It didn't mean anything. He resolved to grow a spine, stop the calls, cut the knot.

Chapter 2

Ararat, Nevada, October 1984

CAL ALBRIGHT PULLED ONTO THE NARROW INCLINE THAT led up to the southwestern Nevada butte whereupon perched the fortified compound called Ararat. There were stone turrets on the uphill side of the road, with machine guns angled through spaces between the stones.

The turrets were unmanned on this chilly night. Security was being provided by the Reverend Joseph Footman's wife, Mia, who was sweeping the front porch of the house.

"Cal," she said. "It's good to see you. And right in time for dinner. I reckon you're starving."

As usual, the reverend's house was full. Cal recognized fellow members of the Council of Eight among the fifteen people around the big oak table. It had been the Council of Seven until Reverend Footman invited Cal to join. He told Cal he had the "youthful energy" that the movement needed. It was quite an honor.

Of course, Cal recognized Richard Shelby, who wore a blue pinstriped suit and had his hair coiffed professionally. He was Reverend Footman's lawyer, and was famous for developing the legal theory that clients whose "national origin" was "Confederate

Southern American" were protected by the US Civil Rights Act of 1964. He leaned heavily on this argument to protect their right to display and wear the Confederate flag, a.k.a. the Stainless Banner, at work and school.

"Kinsmen, we got us a very special guest tonight," the reverend said. Cal thought he was primping Shelby, but then Jackson Yardley came into the room. Everyone stood and applauded.

"Pastor Jack" Yardley had flowing white hair and a light touch. He was past eighty and walked with a silver-handled cane, which he waved at the well-wishers around the table. "Sit down, boys," he said. "And eat up. Keep your priorities in order."

What Cal admired about Pastor Jack was that he had laid his body on the line. He had served seven years in a federal penitentiary for trying to bomb Negroes' school buses back in the sixties, when school integration reached the woods of western North Carolina, where he preached.

"Tell the kinsmen why you're here, Pastor Jack," Reverend Footman said.

"You tell them, Brother Joseph," Yardley said, "while I tear into your wife's most excellent pork chops. My, but they are mouthwatering."

"Pastor Jack and I will be heading to Clyde County tomorrow," Reverend Footman said. "The White Bastion is about to be born."

Cal knew about Clyde County from Pastor Jack's column on LibertyNet, a computer bulletin board that Reverend Footman had gotten someone to set up. Clyde was an almost-empty county, population one thousand and forty-eight, in central Oregon. The county was entirely white to start with. Not that you could trust the sheeple—as Pastor Jack called the majority of his race—to act in their own interests.

An extended family named Pierce was leading the fight, moving up to the county and adding themselves to the voting rolls. The elder of the Pierce clan was running for sheriff and three others for the five-member County Board of Supervisors. It was a lot of Pierces on the ballot, but almost no one voted in Clyde County; the incumbent sheriff had been elected with seventeen votes.

"Revelation 7:4," Reverend Footman called out abruptly to the group.

"'And I heard the number of the sealed, a hundred and forty-four thousand, sealed from every tribe of the sons of Israel,'" someone dutifully intoned. Amens echoed.

"It is not such a big number, a hundred and forty-four thousand. It would be enough to take over the entire Bastion," Footman said.

The man across from Cal asked for the butter to be passed. There was something familiar about him, and Cal tried to place him. His smile was odd, off-center, as if someone had tried to paste it on and missed. Then Cal realized he was the Mendocino County deputy who'd been lynched a year before, just for teasing a colored guy. Some nig had gotten himself arrested while guarding a grow room in the forest. The grow room was superheated and the guard was naked, so the deputy had gotten off a couple of good ones about the size of his Johnson and the animalistic nature of his race.

Two forest rangers on the raid had ratted him out. The Jew radio guy had incited hordes of outraged hippies and other Communists to stampede out of the forest to a public hearing, and the sheriff, who could count, had fired the deputy the following day.

The man was alone when Cal approached him after dinner, before the Council convened. "I live in the County, so I know what they put you through. Cal Albright's my name."

The man blinked rapidly, as if he were processing the information more slowly than it had been offered. "Ernie Fresser," he said. "Thanks."

"It's good to see you here," Cal said.

"I go to the Reverend's Church in Ukiah," Ernie said. "Wanted to see how I could help."

"So where did you land, after?" Ernie looked blank, so Cal added, "I mean, I don't expect getting lynched made it easy to find law enforcement work."

The man smiled dolefully. "I got hired on at Brink's in Santa Rosa," he said. "A kinsman was able to put in a good word. I'm in logistics."

"Well," Cal said. "That could be interesting."

The reverend's deep voice penetrated the hubbub. "Counselors, I must bid you away from the good cheer. I apologize."

"We'll talk," Cal said to Ernie Fresser.

The Council met in Footman's office. One wall was given over to a grainy photograph of a man in aviation combat gear, hoisting a mortar launcher and flashing a big grin. Cal couldn't look at the picture without getting goose bumps. The man was Gordon Kahl, who had been famously at odds with the Internal Revenue Service and with the whole band of traitors, thieves, and whores doing business as the Synagogue of Satan. Kahl slew a couple of federal marshals in self-defense and then, just a year ago, had been gunned down for his beliefs, executed in cold blood in Smithville, Arkansas, by the Zionist Occupied Government that was choking the life out of white America.

"We need bacon, boys," Pastor Jack said. "What's the progress there?" Pastor Jack used his LibertyNet pulpit to stress his conviction that armies marched on their bellies, an insight that he had condensed into the single pork product. He advocated a war chest to fund the full spectrum of insurrectionary needs.

"Sales are up," Footman said. "Thirty percent." He meant the mail-order business of his sermon cassette tapes and Aryan memorabilia. It was small potatoes, Cal thought.

"How is our friend's work progressing?"

It was forbidden, in the name of security, to say the word "counterfeiting" out loud. The friend in question was a small bespectacled man from St. Louis whose code name was Kruger, in honor of Hitler's currency expert who came close to putting the Bank of England out of business. The St. Louis Kruger was a meticulous craftsman with a weakness for boasting, which had resulted in a four-year stint at Leavenworth. He was willing to give it another go, but had become morbidly cautious.

Footman had invested in a Multilith 1640 press, upon which they printed their literature and also Kruger's experiments. These could have passed Cal's eye, but apparently the Feds had higher standards.

"It's moving forward," Footman said. "There's a lot of risk."

Pastor Jack hammered the heel of his silver cane into the ground. "I am going with Brother Joseph to Clyde County, and we will see what we can do to reason with our brethren there, but I confess to you, the Beast is entrenched. It will take more than votes to change the tide."

"You speak my mind," Cal said—a bit boldly, as the newcomer, but he felt restless, ready to act.

"I know I do," Pastor Jack said, "and it has become your time. You and the young lions." Pastor Jack caned his way around the table and stopped in back of Cal. He put his free hand on Cal's shoulder, and Cal could feel heat pulsing from the pastor to himself. "We need dragons of God who know their duty. We called for the government in Le Cesspool Grande to let us be apart from their mongrelism, but to no avail. And now, as we warned, now come the Icemen! Out of the north, out of the frozen lands, once again the giants gather."

Cal wasn't sure about giants gathering, but he had an idea about bacon. Some Weathermen had taken down a Brink's truck a year before, killed three guards, and made off with a million. They'd been caught right away. They were stupid, Communist psychopaths, Cal thought. You did it right, you didn't have to kill anyone and no one would be caught. It was about planning. And having someone on the inside. Like Ernie Fresser.

Chapter 3

San Francisco, October 1984

For several years after Yosh moved north, Spider and Yosh saw each other as often as the hundred and ten miles between them would allow. When he wanted to chill, Spider would sleep over at Yosh's, then hit the road early to fish all day on the Eel River. At night, Yosh would grill the trout and they'd get high and hang.

Then it tapered off. Yosh doubled down, taking his grow indoors, obsessing about his "ladies," as the growers called their female plants. And, Spider thought, his friend was changing, hardening up there in the woods. No one would ever have called Yosh mellow; now, through the radio show, he was tapping into a deep vein of rancor. The station's signal didn't reach San Francisco, but Yosh had all his shows on cassettes and would play his pick hits for Spider during their infrequent visits.

"I know there are anti-Semites out there," Yosh's gravelly voice said from the tape recorder. "I know that you're listening. Why don't you like Jews? Call me up. A frank exchange of views. What are you afraid of? You've got real feelings about this, let 'em out."

"Mr. Steinmetz," a caller's voice said. "Let me ask you a question. Are you a married man?"

"I've spared the ladies that ordeal," Yosh said on the tape.

"Well, let's just say you were. Could you be true to your wife and a girlfriend too?"

"You're going somewhere with this?"

"If you're a Jew, you're not an American. You can't be both. Jews are loyal to the Synagogue of Satan. Fact."

"Indeed."

"Do you see those satellite dishes when you drive on the freeway? They're everywhere. They sit on top of even the most remote farms and ranches. I call them the electronic Jew, with their message of race mixing, running the world as a personal profit machine."

"Interesting insight! Would you care to share your name and organization with us, sir?"

"I am not unaware, sir, that you are an agent of the ZOG."

"Yes, the Zionist Occupied Government, Agent 0 0 Yoshie, you nailed me. Now, if I may, let me ask you a question, sir. Are you masturbating right this second?" Yosh loudly hung up. "Idiot," he said on air. "Cretin. You know what that fool is doing right now? He's whacking off. Ohhhh, I just saved my race on the radio, whack whack whack. Pervert."

"Good stuff, huh?" Yosh said.

"I reckon," Spider said, thinking it was kind of like pulling wings off flies.

It was still good to catch up. They had a date for drinks at Bruno's, an upscale restaurant in the Mission. Yosh said he would pick Spider up at the New People's. He rolled up to the garage in a new, bright red Jeep, with BORN TO BE WILD in florid script on the side.

Caricatures of city hall eminences decorated Bruno's walls. Yosh pushed a small key across the table to Spider.

"What's this?"

"It unlocks my imbecile collection." Yosh explained that his show generated a constant stream of threats which he stuck in a file cabinet and ignored. "Just in case something happens to me," he said. "It'll be someone in this cabinet, guaranteed. You'll just have to figure out who."

"I'm a detective suddenly?"

"I won't be around to complain about your work," Yosh said. They were drinking Hendrick's martinis at Yosh's suggestion. He had developed a taste for the finer things. "Chug it," he said, "if you want another. Julie's coming here at seven."

Julie Choate was Yosh's distributor. She was a radical blonde in her early forties who had multiple sclerosis; she expressed herself politically in a wheelchair, which she often chained to immovable objects, forcing uncomfortable cops to sever the chains and carry her off in front of the television cameras.

"Aaargh," Spider said. A little of Julie's melodrama went a long way as far as he was concerned. He had met her a few times; she always acted like she had bigger fish to fry.

"She's okay," Yosh said. "We go back. And I need her to roll up to the plate now. The lovely SOG is a demanding mistress."

"Sea of Green—SOG to its friends," Yosh clarified. "Hydroponics. Three times the yield. Brave new world. I got to find out how much Julie can handle."

A trill of laughter cascaded from the front of the restaurant. "She makes my teeth hurt," Spider said. They watched the dinner-jacketed maître d' roll Julie Choate toward the table, speaking to her in a low voice while she laughed and threw her head back, exposing a long pale neck.

"We were just talking about you," Yosh said.

"I heard you," she said, and Spider thought *Oh, shit,* until he realized she was joking.

He wondered why she took the risk of moving Yosh's pot. It didn't seem like she would need the money. Her grandfather had been a senator in Connecticut, and she had grown up in Pacific Heights and on various family retreats on the Russian River and Big Sur. Spider thought maybe she sold drugs just to piss off her parents. "I'll let you two talk," he said and got up. No one objected.

It was an exceptionally pleasant fall evening, so Spider chose to walk across town to the occupation at the Filipino Merchant Seamen Hotel in North Beach. He thought it might clear his head.

Of late, he had felt unfocused. His life seemed blurry to him. He had trappings of success he hadn't anticipated and wasn't certain he wanted. He had been sexually implicated with numerous women, but the very occasional ones he thought he might get serious about had proven more complicated than he could handle. He was thirty-four, locked into second gear, needing to shift. He walked past Ganim's deli, with its Palestinian poster in the window. Suicide bombers were starting to blow themselves up, in Palestine and on American planes and in the American embassy in Beirut and elsewhere. The images of the bombers in the paper reminded Spider of the way the Viet Cong looked, even when they were about to be executed. Especially when they were about to be executed. Defiant. Believers. Way more into their cause than he was into his.

Over the course of nine years, San Francisco's political vortex had inhaled Spider. Rallies, demos, agitprop theater, meetings, occupations, benefits—these were the stuff of life in the City, along with drug-fueled parties to recover from all of the foregoing.

The American economy was trending positive again, or so the papers said. America had kicked Grenada's ass, and San Francisco was the queen of the Pacific Rim. You could get a pain au chocolate just about everywhere. Downtown was expanding into the Tenderloin, into South of Market, and into Chinatown and North Beach.

Very specifically, downtown had expanded to encompass the Filipino Merchant Seamen Hotel, on Kearny Street, and Spider was headed there to link arms in a position of maximum tensile rigidity and impedance. The goal was to make it hard for the sheriff's deputies to haul them out of the hotel, a decrepit building in a prime location. Spider gave his name to a monitor, who checked him off a list and gestured him inside.

The developer had played a slow and clenching hand. He had followed all the rules, and now he had a federal judge's promise to hold the county's liberal sheriff in contempt if he didn't implement the evictions.

When the deputies came at midnight, it was all over very quickly. Their linkages of maximum impedance proved irrelevant. No one wanted to hurt or be hurt. The deputies were younger than Spider, with buzz cuts, on affectless best behavior. They carried out the protestors like slabs of beef. After a certain symbolic distance, there wasn't very much point that Spider could see in being carried. "Okay," he said. "I'll walk."

The deputies put him down and watched to make sure he kept on walking. He heard, above him, a familiar voice saying, through a bullhorn, "This is not acceptable. I will not accept it." He knew even before he looked that it would be Julie, and that her positioning would be precarious—eye candy for the news cameras.

She was on a second-floor balcony and had chained her wheelchair to the balustrade. In an excellent Julie touch, the balcony itself was quite palpably listing. It looked like it might collapse at any instant, spilling her into the crowd milling below. *Our own suicide bomber*, Spider thought, and then thought himself mean for thinking it. He made himself pay attention to her speech about gentrification and class struggle and international solidarity.

A deputy with a chain cutter appeared at her side. She had been known to assault agents of law enforcement, but this time, mindful perhaps of the balcony's flawed construction, she let the deputy hack his way through the chain unmolested. Then two deputies picked up her chair, and she disappeared from view.

Chapter 4

THE SOUNDTRACK OF CLACKING DEADBOLTS WERE JUST WHITE noise to Siobhan by now. She had fixed up her Lower East Side apartment the way she liked it—minimal, no clutter. The neighborhood was still tense, but no longer a total war zone. Little galleries and restaurants were edging east from SoHo and the Village. Siobhan enjoyed the social afflatus of having been a pioneer, in place since the early days of 1982.

What she no longer liked, number one: her job. At first, it had been a dream come through, a vindication of propelling herself from the soft Phoenix life to the vigor and rigor of New York. She got to fight for the environment, as a lawyer with a firm that researched and filed class actions. And at a woman-led firm, as its promotional literature boasted.

And what a woman! What a sanctimonious, close-minded, absolute prima donna, ruling the roost as managing partner. Preening her favorites. Demeaning the others. "Pay attention, Siobhan, you might learn something." Smugly quoting her own previous dicta: "As I said after the Peabody case in '79, though apparently no one was listening…"

The managing partner was famously assertive on the front line of social struggle. Siobhan could no longer look at her or hear her voice without irritation.

What Siobhan no longer liked, number two: her boyfriend, Mel. Not out of bed, anyway.

It had started so promisingly two years before, at CBGB's. She had gone to see the Bad Brains, a punk reggae group that Isabel, a younger and far hipper coworker, had touted as "unbelievable live." She realized her mistake as soon as she entered the club. She had felt old before, but it had never been so in her face. Here, the dancing involved pogoing on the stage and jumping into a mosh pit, counting on being caught, and not always being correct in that assumption. Siobhan had decided to have a drink and just listen to the music. She was leaning against a wall in the back, when an exaggeratedly slender guy approached her.

"Want to dance?" the slender fellow said. "I can throw you off the stage."

He had sandy hair, just starting to recede, which was cut in a conservative, preppy style. He looked completely out of place and completely at ease.

"I can throw *you* off the stage," Siobhan said, but gave him a smile to encourage his bravado.

They chatted and discovered that they lived within two blocks of each other. But Mel didn't live in a rent decontrolled building. He lived in a squat, an abandoned wreck on Avenue C called Elephant House.

Mel was a computer programmer, just turned twenty-seven, six years younger than she was. They argued about rent decontrol. Mel adduced examples of old women and cripples being forced into the streets by landlords eager to rent to people like Siobhan and carve the East Village out of Loisaida, which is what the Puerto Ricans and Mel called the area.

They jabbed till the next set. While the band tuned, Mel said, "I like the way you don't take any shit. Why don't we hang out sometime?" No man had ever come on to her in quite that way.

She accepted his invitation to dine at the squat two nights later. When she arrived, there were people taking turns on an Osborne computer. Mel showed Siobhan that they were logged into a network called The Grapevine, where simultaneous conversations concerning just about everything imaginable were taking place. People sent messages to each other using their computers and something called a modem, which translated the words into electronic signals and then back to words on the recipient computer. Siobhan's law firm had computers, but she'd never seen anything like this.

"Where did you get this?" she asked Mel.

He pointed to his forehead. It was his baby; he had written the code and shared it with whomever wanted to join.

After dinner, he invited her to sample the squat's home-distilled plum brandy on the tenement's roof. They had a fire pit up there and lounge chairs, the circumference secured by barbed wire strung eight feet high.

"There's a plum in here, you say?" Siobhan said. It smelled and tasted like rubbing alcohol.

"Absolutely," Mel said. "The best plum one can possibly scavenge."

It was bearable in medicinal sips. "How did you end up here?" Siobhan asked.

"Grew up in Greenwich. Phillips Exeter. Yale. Acid," he said. "And here I am."

She took this in. "Spend the night with me?" he said.

"Sure," she said.

•••

In bed, Mel was innovative and tireless. It was the best night she'd had for quite a while. She was thirty-three and wanted to have children. Mel intrigued her. He called the next day. "Care for canapés and cocktails at the Century Club?"

Mel told her the City had just published a master housing plan for Loisaida that credited the sweat equity of qualifying squats. It was a fabulous victory, the first time the City had acknowledged the squatters' movement. Important people were suddenly interested in hearing Mel's views at nice restaurants.

Siobhan found it entertaining, for a few months, to ride shotgun. It took her a while to figure out that Mel had but one speed: overdrive. He was on the radio browbeating the Department of Housing Preservation and Development, or appropriating phone lines and electric cables for the squat's use, or planning the Global Squatters' Congress, or marching in rallies to get the police out of Tompkins Square, or settling disputes at the Grapevine, or dining out as the celebrity squatter, or cooking up his pasta mysterioso back at Elephant House.

But they never actually had what could be called a conversation. He might ask a handful of rapid-fire questions about her legal cases, but she could tell his heart wasn't in it; it was just something he'd learned to do, so people wouldn't think he was self-absorbed.

He was completely self-absorbed, she'd realized. He was so self-absorbed that he didn't seem to realize she had broken up with him.

To be fair, this might have to do with the fact that every third or fourth time he called and asked if he could come over, she said, "I suppose." And then, like last night, they'd drink some wine, and he would talk about the conspiracy to spatially deconcentrate low-income communities. Then they would have plausible sex and she would tell him that she wanted to wake up alone, and he would agree, saying it would help him get an early start on things the next day.

Siobhan picked up an empty wine bottle and dressed for work. She disengaged her Rubik's Cube of locks and then reengaged them on the outside.

It was nice on the street, still late spring, the sidewalks not yet succumbing to summer's torpor. It was the kind of day when it felt like a privilege to walk to work, from Loisaida to the managing partner's brownstone in the West Village, which she charged the firm a top-of-market rate to rent.

"What's new and interesting? Or at least new," Siobhan said to Isabel. Siobhan had started with Isabel's job and moved up. Now Isabel fielded the incoming calls and parceled them out to the trial lawyers, tap dancing around office politics. She was in her final year of law school at NYU and aspired to become Siobhan in a couple of years.

"You're going to like this, girlfriend," Isabel said. She gave Siobhan a folder. "Californ-i-ay. Wahoo."

"That's Texas," Siobhan said. In the folder was the form her firm used when a new lead came in. Under "Source of Lead," Isabel had typed "Online Network: Grapevine." That was intriguing. Siobhan had become devoted to the Grapevine through Mel, and she had infected Isabel with her enthusiasm, taking pleasure in clueing her younger colleague to something hip.

A Grapeviner in Ukiah had uploaded a newspaper report that Redwood Pacific Lumber company, headed by the notorious union-busting Bill Ricci, had been spraying poison on the gyppos, their contract labor force. The poison was meant to destroy the junk trees so the gyppo lumber crews could get at the bigger timber. "I swig it at public events," a company spokesman was quoted as saying. "It tastes like sarsaparilla."

It was supposedly the third documented instance of Garlon being sprayed on a Redwood Pacific gyppo crew. Isabel had contacted the reporter, who had been glad to provide a list of local contacts.

It felt like a long shot to Siobhan. Class action law was very specific, and this sounded more like a bunch of personal injury claims. Too bad. She'd been to Disneyland a bunch of times with her dad, but she'd never been to the Bay Area.

She only thought about Spider at odd moments. Like now. She expected he was doing fine. The word was that being a straight male in San Francisco was like shooting fish in a barrel.

There was a memo on her desk from the managing partner's secretary, informing her that quarterly reports were due the next day by 10:00 a.m. *sharp.* Siobhan could hear the managing partner saying the word.

Siobhan thought about San Francisco again, and about Spider. He was history, but at this particular New York moment, appealing history. Of course, his comical breakups notwithstanding, the likelihood of Spider being available in San Francisco was remote. For some reason, her memory turned to the fine mesh of scars that covered the muscles of his back. It suddenly intrigued her to find out if Spider were at liberty. She looked up the number of his garage and dialed. A man with a Scandinavian accent answered, and then she heard the sound of an extension cord flopping and the guy saying, "Spider, for you." Then she heard a rolling sound and his voice saying, "Hello."

She'd thought carefully of how to broach it. He wasn't stupid. If he wanted her to stay with him, he'd figure out a way to say so.

"Spider," she said, "it's Siobhan. I'm riding out your way to rescue the gyppos." She told him briefly what the case was about.

"Cool," Spider said. He seemed to take the news calmly. "So where are you staying?"

She didn't say anything. The silence hung.

"I mean," he finally said, "You could stay here."

That could mean a spare room, Siobhan thought. Spider was not known for his sumptuous decor. She envisioned lying on a mattress on the floor of an otherwise empty room, while Spider and his mate cavorted loudly in the master bedroom.

"And your girlfriend," Siobhan said. "Where will she be?"

"Teen lingerie models' convention in Paris," Spider said. "She'll age out after this year, so she didn't want to miss it." She almost bit, and then remembered that Spider liked to assert outlandish fake facts with a straight face. It could be annoying or it could be funny, or both.

"You're still an asshole, Spider Lacey," she said. Then she started laughing at almost being taken in. She knew her laugh amused him. "I accept your gracious offer."

Chapter 5

Ukiah, Tuesday, June 11, 1985

CAL ALBRIGHT LIKED TO PARK OUTSIDE BILL RICCI'S mansion and sit a minute every time he was invited over. The lumber baron resided in three stories of blocky, ornate grandeur, surrounded by oak and madrone, set way back on a hundred and sixty acres. It was modeled on the Palazzo Farnese in Rome, the third floor of which Michelangelo himself had designed for Alessandro Farnese, just elected pope at the 1534 conclave. Ricci called it Farnese Mio.

Cal heard Guido, Bill Ricci's cook, crooning *La Bohème* through the open kitchen window. After a half-dozen visits, he had come to feel almost at home visiting Farnese Mio. But he still marveled at how fast his life had changed.

Just two years ago, he had been thirty-one, with a wife with screwed-up plumbing. She chopped up dates and made a poultice, which he really didn't really like to think about. There was a powder made out of chasteberry and maca root, which she had read in a magazine was a "proven remedy." Their little house smelled like a swamp. When Cal came home from hacking down redwoods, she would give him his dinner and then lie on her back and invite him to plant his son inside her. He had been in despair, living in a nation where patriots were running out of time. His kids would grow up second-class in their own country. If he could even have kids.

Then he had happened upon Reverend Footman's Church of Jesus Christ, Christian and blessings multiplied. The reverend's very first sermon had broken a dam in Cal's mind. He could remember it to this day. "Our leaders in the false Christian clergy tell us there must be a middle in the road. But I want you to know that God has no use, absolutely no use, for the middle, for you are neither hot or cold in the middle, and God said He would spew you out of His mouth."

In a church study group, he read *The Turner Diaries*, an inspirational novel about race war, a hijacked nuclear arsenal, and the victory of the white race. It didn't seem that far-fetched to Cal, especially after his wife finally managed to get pregnant and he started thinking some more about the world his son would inherit. He started talking to his fellow gyppo loggers. A lot of them felt the same way he did. Then he met Bill Ricci, who gave a talk at the church's speaker series.

Ricci was in the papers a lot. He was known for his spirited attacks on the environmentalists who were starting to stick their pointy little heads above the ground, talking about old-growth redwoods and spotty owls, which they considered much more important than anyone's right to make a living. Ricci wasn't partial to unions either. Or Communists, same thing.

"Mr. Ricci?" Cal had said, when the speaker called for questions. Ricci smiled at Cal from the rostrum.

"Those were powerful words, sir," Cal said. "I thought you would like to know that a lot of people like me who work for you agree with you."

Ricci peered at him. "You work for Redwood? I don't recognize you."

"We've never met. I'm a logger. And not a union logger either."

"A gyppo!"

Cal inclined his head modestly, and then said, "We need to organize behind these ideas, sir. We need to take this country back."

Ricci had thanked him and moved to the next question, but when the question period was over and people were starting to disperse, Cal heard a voice say, "Young man!" Ricci drew close and put a friendly arm around his shoulder. "Come back to the house," he said. "I'll throw a steak into you, and you can tell me what things are really like down where the work gets done."

At Farnese Mio, Cal had listened politely as the older man poured different cognacs and discoursed on their respective grapes. They all tasted pretty much the same to Cal; he didn't really like to drink. He could see that Ricci was drawn to him, though, and wondered where it all was going.

After the second fat-bottomed snifter, Ricci had suggested that Cal come to work for him, take charge of contracting at scale with the gyppos, so that Ricci could teach the unions one last, cataclysmic lesson. Cal said he would like that very much.

By the fourth snifter, the two men were sentimental. They spoke to each other of their love of the West, of the forest and the ocean, of the birds and the fish and the game.

"Mr. Ricci," Cal said.

"Son?" Ricci said. It sounded like he meant the word quite literally.

"This should be white people's country, sir. We should claim it. Ten percent, that's fair, right? And some Canada." Cal's face felt flushed, but the words came tumbling out. "Washington, Oregon, Idaho, Wyoming, Western Montana, Northern California, Northwestern Colorado, Northern Utah, Alaska, British Columbia, Alberta, Yukon and the Northwest Territories."

"It's already white people," Cal said. "Ninety-nine percent. Our bastion. We'd let the Jews and coloreds have the rest."

Ricci had smiled broadly. Then he realized Cal was dead serious and erased his smile. He raised his glass to his new friend and said, "To the bastion."

•••

EXCEPT FOR THE MEMORABLE FIRST OCCASION, CAL HAD always been one of a group of men. "An intimate dinner party among friends," Ricci liked to call these stag evenings, which invariably devolved to loud reminiscences, dominated by Ricci, not fit for ladies.

This time, Ricci had told Cal he wanted to talk something over, "just the two of us." He welcomed Cal and ushered him into the cavernous living room. He mixed their drinks himself. Cal was about to wish his host good health when Ricci raised a silencing finger. Guido was about to hit an unrestrained high note in the kitchen. Cal grunted his appreciation.

"How's the good work on the bastion going, Cal?" Ricci asked him.

The question surprised Cal. Ricci had never brought up the bastion after their first meeting, and neither had Cal.

Beyond the question itself, Ricci's whole manner was odd. He was an erect sixty-four-year-old who sponsored yacht races and tennis tournaments and escorted tall blondes at international powerfests. But he looked kind of distracted tonight.

"We're plugging away, Mr. Ricci," he said, "Getting the word out, trying to raise awareness, you know." Ricci looked blank, as if he didn't know what Cal was talking about. "How are things with you?"

"Oh, well," Ricci said, making a small gesture to take in the grandeur of his abode. "I can't complain."

Cal knew that wasn't true. Redwood Pacific was Mendocino County's biggest employer, and word got around.

Guido entered with cantaloupe wrapped in home-slaughtered and cured prosciutto. Ricci seized his retainer's wrist and asked him to detail the family history and personal foibles of the swine who was participating so selflessly in their repast. His buoyancy struck Cal as forced, a valiant effort to rise above the tragic exterior siding saga.

Reducing junk trees and redwood saplings to sawdust and then mashing the dust into particle board for interior use had made Ricci beloved by Wall Street and his board of directors. Two years before, he had decided to reach for the much larger market for weatherproof exterior siding. The new product passed all internal inspections and was launched, sweeping away the field. But after two winters of use, a consistent pattern of leaks and mold appeared. Lawsuits proliferated.

When something lousy happened to Bill Ricci, Yosh Steinmetz made sure it didn't stay a secret. Steinmetz dug up some Ricci garbage for every show. The Egret Lagoon episode, a year before, had driven Steinmetz berserk. Ricci owned a patch of land the State needed in order to complete a park. Ricci had extracted twice the market value, plus renaming the Egret to William A. Ricci Lagoon. Steinmetz had retaliated with a segment called *Billy Ricci Time*, with the *Howdy Doody* melody tinkling in the background.

Last week, Steinmetz had gone off on Ricci for banging a starlet while his wife was being treated for depression. You might despise Steinmetz for the Jew scum he was, but you still listened. Everyone listened.

"How do you do it, Mr. R.?" Cal said. "Stay so positive. I would squeal like a stuck pig if that radio guy said that stuff about me. Lying Hebrew."

Ricci seemed lost in thought. "It wasn't depression, you know. It was dementia. She was gone and wasn't coming back. Was I supposed to frame my dick and hang it on the wall in memoriam?"

Over dinner, Ricci maundered. He talked about his father, who beat him, and about his son, who disappointed him. He bemoaned the new breed of business executives with their MBAs and soft hands. He admired his own hands—manicured now, but still sinewy and strong. Cal wondered what Ricci had brought him here to talk about. They were on coffee and cigars when Ricci got it out.

"That Jewish radio fellow," he said. It was the first time Cal could remember him talking about someone being Jewish, and, right away, he knew where Ricci was going. "He's hurting me," Ricci said. "He's hurting the company. He's hurting everyone who does business with the company." He looked hard at Cal. "Or works for the company."

Cal figured Ricci wanted him to volunteer. "He's like all of them," Cal said.

"Well, this particular one," Ricci said, "is the one who's hurting me and the company and its employees."

Cal wanted to raise his hand, but the timing was poor. In two days, Cal intended to ambush a Brink's truck on the Calpella grade and relieve it of as much as a million dollars for the cause. Much as he appreciated Mr. Ricci's patronage, he really didn't want to be distracted from his mission. It wasn't easy saying no to Ricci, but he couldn't say yes. Not right this moment. Not until he could plan things properly.

"You wish something would happen to him," Cal said. Ricci stared at him.

"I'd be grateful," Ricci said. "I remember my friends." When Cal didn't say anything, Ricci added, "Loyalty is important to me, Cal."

"You've been good to me, Mr. Ricci," Cal said. "Let me give this some serious thought."

Chapter 6

San Francisco, Friday, June 14

Spider arrived at SFO way early to meet Siobhan's plane. He ordered a scotch in an airport bar. He ordered another and his tongue started to feel big. He ordered a double espresso. The admixture felt like chalk and cheese in his esophagus. He made his way to Siobhan's arrival gate and stood at the back of the greeting throng, watching the first passengers disembark. Suddenly, he figured it out. She'd become some sort of grotesque, reaching out to Spider because no one else would have her.

She'd put on a hundred pounds.

She would be in a wheelchair, a supersized quadriplegic testing his love.

Spider made a conscious effort to pull his thoughts together, even as he steeled himself for Siobhan jelly-rolling off the plane. He closed his eyes to center himself, and when he opened them, she was standing before him, looking quizzical. She hadn't expanded any, but had cut off her hair. Just about all of it.

"Wow," he said. "Your hair." She didn't say anything. He realized more was called for. "You look," he said, "amazing. Give me a second."

"Do you really think so?" she said. "Of course you do, and if you didn't, you're smart enough not to say so, right?"

"I think so," Spider said. They hadn't touched. "Do we shake hands now?"

All around them, happy families and couples exchanged fleshy welcomes. "Why don't we hug?" Siobhan said. "People do that a lot at airports. There would be plausible deniability."

"Okay," Spider said. "That sounds pretty good to me." He remained inert.

"I always have to do everything," Siobhan said, and embraced him with her arms around his back. She started to kiss him, but then turned her face away. "Eww," she said. He realized his breath was toxic.

"Sorry about that. Had a little something to calm down, and then another little something to regain consciousness."

She put her hands on his shoulders, like she had the first time they'd met, and scrutinized him carefully. He wasn't sure what she saw.

"Want to get something to eat?" he said.

He took her from the airport to Ric's Tahitian Paradise nearby, in San Bruno. Ric was a passionate ichthyologist who had sailed the Seven Seas and captured, eaten, or incarcerated a substantial percentage of their inhabitants. An awestruck account of Ric's adventures, authored by Ric, occupied three pages of the folio style menu. From a series of enormous fish tanks on each wall, Ric's captives peered impassively, like hitmen evaluating their targets.

Their waiter looked somewhat crustacean himself, with a long face and flat, pasted-down blond mustache. They ordered two lobsters and wine, Siobhan spending more time over the wine list than she used to.

She knew her way around a lobster. As they ate, she told him all about the gyppos' suffering. "It's conceivably grounds for a class action," she said. "Perhaps. And I was feeling curious about you. It's been a long time."

"Really?" Spider said.

"Ten years," she said.

"I know," he said. "You were curious?"

She didn't answer right away, and then she said, "Yes, I believe so." It was as good as he was going to get, he could see.

"Oh, while it crosses my mind," Spider said. "Are you single?"

"I am, Spider," she said. "Is there a reason you ask?"

"Just sort of leveling the playing field," he said. "Pay no attention. So, what's your plan? It's not a vacation, I guess."

"Research," she said. "I've got to spend time in some place called Ukiah, lure the lonesome gyppos out of the forest to talk to me."

"Ukiah," Spider said. "If you want company, I'd take you. My friend lives there. We could stay with him if..." Spider paused. He was most definitely getting ahead of himself.

"If we like sleeping together again?" she said. "Well, we might as well see about that."

She was always a step ahead of him.

"Okay," he said. "Their desserts are shitty anyway."

On the way out to the car, he slowed down to extract his car keys. She poked him hard in the ribs and said, "Get a move on, will ya."

He felt suddenly shy with her.

•••

SPIDER'S BEDROOM FEATURED A KING-SIZED BED AND A large tapestry of Ganesh, the Indian elephant god, that someone had foisted on him in lieu of payment for a carburetor overhaul. Spider liked the tusky, sloe-eyed deity standing guard.

The centerpiece of the living room was a leather sofa shaped like a wide horseshoe. Spider had outfitted it with casters so it could be rolled toward either the vinyl appreciation zone or the sports and movie perusal domain. Spider's music came in the form of 33 1/3 LPs, not cassette tapes and certainly not these new CDS that made the music sound like it had been produced by robots.

The sports and movie zone centered on a twenty-seven inch Trinitron, which Ohanian termed Spider's nonrefundable, irreversible, official one-way ticket into the bourgeoisie. But Spider noticed that Ohanian practically wore a hole into the sofa, getting high with Spider and watching ballgames and *Honeymooners* reruns on the VCR. The VCR was Spider's big leap into technological modernity. He had hated advertising for as long as he could remember, and he took pleasure in forwarding through the ads.

In the opening of the horseshoe couch sat a massive oak coffee table, the repository of whatever Spider was eating, drinking, reading, and smoking. Also on the table was the controller of a wired remote control system that Spider had rigged up. A spaghetti nest of wires snaked across the shaggy brown rug, but it was a small price to pay for the pleasure of fast-forwarding through commercials.

At the room's far end was a small bookshelf. He didn't read much. He had some political books, gifts from girlfriends who thought he could stand some consciousness improvement. He would read a chapter or two while the affair was in progress. On Ohanian's recommendation, he had just started a novel about the fast life in New York. It was funny enough, but it could have been about China or the moon for its relevance to him. It centered on people who snorted cocaine all the time. Spider wondered if Siobhan was in that world now.

Siobhan inspected the flat without comment. He had bought some tulips and gladioli and some champagne. He put two wineglasses on the table, wishing he had flutes. He felt self-conscious, aware of how few books he owned. He felt like she was measuring the arc of his life. "I just sublet this from a friend," Spider said. "It's all his stuff."

"It's very Spider classic," she said, declining the bait. "Love the wiring." She threw the champagne back and ducked into the bathroom. He drank his champagne, listening to the shower run. She was wearing his robe when she came out. When other women did that, they looked like Droopy the dwarf. She took the glass out of his hand and said, "Your turn, kiddo. Brush your teeth."

Spider showered quickly and brushed his teeth assiduously. She was under his covers when he came out. Her empty diaphragm case was on the bed table.

She could see how excited he was, and she toyed with him, prolonging matters till he thought he'd burst. She seemed to know when he was on the verge and would slacken her attentions just in time. He brought her to orgasm with his mouth and then his fingers, and when she brought him inside of her, he couldn't contain himself, worse than a high school kid.

She got up naked to bring in the last of the champagne. He felt as lost in love as ever.

"I guess I can still just about tolerate being in bed with you," she said. She traced with her fingertip the scars on his back. Neither of them spoke for a while until she said, "Tell me about our Ukiah host."

"Yosh has kind of taken root up there in the woods," Spider said. "He grows pot and does a talk show on the community radio station. He's a star. He can froth at the mouth as much as he wants, and he does. People eat it up."

"How did you meet him?"

"At a party, just after I came out here. Just after you went out there."

"Didn't you ever want to visit?"

He covered her body with his in lieu of answering.

Chapter 7

Calpella Grade, Friday, June 14, 1985

CAL LOOKED AT ERNIE FRESSER SHOVELING IN HIS bacon and eggs. Ernie wasn't exactly a prize specimen, in Cal's opinion. He had been useful, for sure, picking up from chatter in the Brink's office that once every two months a Brink's truck loaded up cash in Lakeport, Clear Lake, and other small towns between Highways 5 and 101, then headed west on State Route 20 over the Calpella grade toward Santa Rosa. Ernie had heard drivers talking about downshifting all the way to get through the Mayacamas Mountains. Cal had taken it from there, driving out to the grade and discovering that it was not only steep, but on a jug handle that arched around the widest part of the mountain. The furthest part of the handle was hidden from traffic anywhere else on the road. It was perfect.

Ernie was not perfect. He talked way too much when he drank, and he drank often. "Ernie," Cal said. "Remember to act normal at work."

"I know that," Ernie said with his mouth full. "You don't need to keep reminding me." He banged his fork and knife down on his plate.

"Hey," Cal said to change the subject, "Guess who wants a little job done?" Ernie made some futile guesses. "How about Mr. Ricci asking me to take care of Steinmetz," Cal said. "The radio guy?"

"I know who he is," Ernie said. The Jew had gloated on the air after Ernie was fired by the sheriff. "And so we say goodbye to Deputy Ernie Fresser who is insignificant and doesn't matter a rat's ass. What matters is the message we send to racists...."

"I'll take care of it," Ernie said. "I'd like that."

"But not right now, Bunyan," Cal said, using Ernie's code name. "We're talking a million, maybe more, in just a few hours. Every cop in three counties will be on the road after we're done. We got to stay focused. Lay low."

"Yeah," Ernie said. Then he added, "Out where he lives, be hardly nothing to it."

"But first things first, right?" Cal said.

"Right," Ernie said.

•••

CAL FELT NERVOUS, ALL HIS SENSES ALIVE. It was two in the afternoon and he was in the turnout on the jug handle of the Calpella grade. He had positioned two signalmen fore and aft, to keep traffic at bay while a "work crew" maneuvered a tree off the road up ahead on the jug handle.

Cal tried to keep his breath even and his pulse steady as he sat in the old Ford Econoline van, newly purchased with a fake ID, awaiting an incoming call from Robert E. on his CB radio. They all had code names. Cal's was Earl, for Earl Turner of *The Turner Diaries*. A lot had gone into getting to this moment. In just a few minutes, he would start to change history.

"Robert E. here. A terrific day," the voice said on the designated CB frequency. That meant the Brink's truck had rolled out of the

Lakeport gas station and would be on State Route 20 in five minutes and at the jug handle in seventeen.

"No little Indians," Robert E. said a few minutes later. That was great news. It meant the Brink's truck had the road to itself, except for Robert E., who was trailing a discreet distance behind. Yah was on the job.

Ten minutes later Cal gave an order over the CB and his signalmen uphill and downhill prepared to set up stanchions and orange off-limits tape as soon as the truck passed. The signalmen were decked out in oversized hardhats, huge walkie-talkie headsets bracketing their faces to hide their features. When asked, the men were to say a big pine had come down around the turn, almost massacred a family from Iowa.

Cal could hear the truck, in its lowest gear, straining around the bend. The truck shuddered to a halt as it encountered Odin's van athwart the road. Thor, armed with an H&K .308 caliber semi-automatic rifle, jumped out of one side of the van while Utah emerged from the backseat, brandishing a hand-lettered sign that said GET OUT OR DIE.

The driver and his partner cowered behind their bulletproof glass but made no signs of moving. That was what the jacketed shells in the .308 were for. Odin blew out a corner of the supposedly bulletproof window. Shards of glass strafed the truck's cab, and instantly the two Brink's men were out of the cab with their hands up.

That left the third guard in the back with the money, and they turned their attention there, only noticing belatedly that the driver, in his terror, had neglected to set the emergency brake. The truck was rolling gently toward the edge of the road and the steep embankment below. Cal acted fast, firing two shots into the tires from his Smith and Wesson 9mm pistol. Then, Odin shot a hole in the side of the truck with the .308, which got the other guard out and the cash compartment opened.

Listening to the police band on his CB, Cal heard no unusual activity until a woman's voice came on, saying she was in a traffic stop on the Capella grade and had just heard what sounded an awful lot like shots.

"Where are you, exactly?" the voice on the sheriff's side asked.

The woman wasn't entirely sure.

"You're at a traffic stop? What kind of stop?" the deputy asked.

It took several minutes for the woman to figure out her location and to inform the policeman that they were stopped because of tree work around the bend.

Cal could hear the deputy yelling to someone, "There any tree work scheduled on twenty West?" Cal figured they had a safe fifteen minutes before they sorted things out and got moving. He spoke into his radio and said, "Those ain't shots, that's tree limbs snapping," giving the deputies another reason to mosey.

They were about a third of the way through transferring the bags from the truck to their vans. "Faster," Cal said. He was covering the guards and driver, face down on the ground. The men loaded for ten more minutes, leaving some bags on board the Brink's; Cal was disciplined. Then they jumped in their trucks and headed back up the grade.

Safe in the forest, they counted their haul. When he got to a million with most of the bags remaining, Cal felt spiritual. When he got to three million and three hundred thousand, he felt like he could fly.

•••

DANIEL BEN-HORIN

Ernie Fresser hunkered over his desk, listening to the hubbub from the dispatchers' area. Somebody turned up the radio, and they all listened to the breaking news: A truck had been held up at gunpoint on the Calpella grade. Driver suffered lacerations from flying glass, might lose an eye. Millions taken.

Ernie was bursting inside, proud to be getting his own back, wanting to jump on his desk and let out a yell.

He couldn't do that. He couldn't even tell his wife, Suzie. His getting fired as a deputy had been a blow to her, both the humiliation and losing the health insurance. She would stand by her man, but he knew she was disappointed. She wouldn't want him taking any chances.

It still rankled Ernie the way Cal had hammered home the need to maintain his routine and betray no emotion. It occurred to Ernie, and not for the first time, that Cal didn't respect his intelligence. As Ernie drove home, he imagined how he might sort of let Suzie know without really letting her know. Cal said it was the most selfish, despicable thing imaginable to tell someone you loved something that could only hurt them. But maybe he could get away with saying, when the news came on, "Imagine being married to one of the guys who did that."

Ernie heard the TV when he was still in the driveway. His mood darkened. His daughter, Jen, was only six, but she loved her sitcoms. For Ernie, it was like letting the enemy into your living room.

He heard George Jefferson being uppity as usual, and Louise and Lionel trying to get him to calm down. He went directly to the TV and turned off the sound. "Honey," he said to Jen, "those aren't our people. We'll find you something else to watch. Hey, lookit, the nature channel—now that's real. Lookit that lion, honey, and there's an antelope." Jen screamed as the lion did unto the antelope what lions do to antelopes.

They had dinner together—hush puppies with minced hot dogs, which they all loved—and then Ernie said he and Jen would watch TV while Suzie cleaned up. His wife gave him a warning look. He knew she thought he took the shows too seriously, but he couldn't help it. Big Bird and his own namesake, Ernie, for example, drove him crazy with their Communist ideas. Mr. Rogers was a queer. The Jews ran entertainment and the coloreds did the singing and dancing.

He liked Tom and Jerry, though. Father and daughter laughed as Mammy Two-Shoes bemoaned her rodent problem in her thick Negro voice. Then an episode of *Alvin and the Chipmunks,* and then it was time to start Jen's march toward bed.

From the kitchen, Suzie called, "Don't get her too wound up or she won't sleep."

The game Ernie played with his daughter before she went to bed was uncomplicated. He hid somewhere, she found him, he roared, she screamed and ran to her mommy.

Jen hopped from one foot to the other, saying, "Hide, Daddy, hide." There were only a few hiding places in the small house: one of the three closets, the shower stall, or under the bed, which was not very comfortable and also presented difficulties in terms of leaping out and roaring. The little yard was just a lawn with a miniature playhouse—no hidey holes there.

"Seven Heavenly Angels," Jen said, counting in the kitchen. "Eight Heavenly Angels."

Ernie went into the tiny room they used for storage. A love seat pushed against the wall was covered with periodicals and books. On a whim, Ernie pulled the love seat away from the wall and lay down behind it. Aryan lore fell off the top of the pile and blanketed him.

It would take her quite a while to find him, he thought. He would enjoy the respite. He heard his daughter checking the usual spots.

"I can't find him, Mommy," Jen said. "Help me." She gave up too easily, he thought. He lifted the rear end of the love seat with his foot and let it bang down on the floor.

"Have you looked in the little room, sweetheart?" Suzie said, picking up the hint.

"He's not there!"

"Well, look again, honey. Mommy's got a hunch."

Ernie heard them both come into the room. They looked in the closet, and then Suzie said, "Did you look behind the love seat?"

Ernie was into it now. When Jen poked her head over the back of the love seat, he jumped up, spouting spumes of lore, and cut loose with a roar that made her jump back, screaming with terror. She landed on the floor, scraping her elbow and switching to cries of pain.

Suzie bundled her up in her arms, cutting Ernie a reproachful glance. Ernie followed them into the kitchen and enveloped them both in a bear hug. "You scared me, Daddy," Jen said, but she was smiling through her tears.

While Suzie tucked her in, Ernie flipped through the dial waiting for the news. The public television station was running a documentary on immigration. Smiling mud-colored announcers said Hispanics would be the majority in California by 2020.

"Bad daddy," Suzie said, joining him on the couch, but she was smiling.

Ernie put his arm around Suzie and drew her toward him. He nuzzled into the crook of her neck, caressing her breast with his hand.

"Ernie," she said, squirming away. "Stop. She's still awake."

Ernie went to the door of their daughter's bedroom and peeked in. He closed the door behind him and whispered to Suzie, "Out like a light." Then he gave a *sotto voce* roar, mimicking the one he'd laid on Jen. Suzie made a gesture of mock fright. He enveloped her in his arms and carried her to bed.

After they made love, he asked how would she feel about a little spur-of-the-moment camping trip up to Clear Lake. Cook some steaks, toast some marshmallows with Jen? They didn't get out enough, enjoy the beautiful country God had given them.

She leaned her head on his shoulder and said she'd love that. Ernie felt great, but then remembered he was supposed to join the guys in the forest that evening. "Oh," he said.

"What?" Suzie said, smiling up at him.

"Nothing," Ernie said. The guys would be there for a few days. He'd join them after getting back from Clear Lake. Cal wouldn't like it, but too bad.

Part Two

Chapter 8

Ukiah, Saturday, June 15

THE DEPUTY SPIDER REACHED BY PHONE FROM THE Circle K said to wait right there. Spider rejoined Siobhan in the Citroën. The headline of the *Ukiah Daily Journal* in the coin box said "Death on the Tarmac." The Arabs had struck again, hijacking a TWA flight, killing a soldier and throwing his body from the plane in the Beirut airport. The world felt dire.

"I've never seen a dead body," Siobhan said, "except in a casket."

To Spider, she looked like she was working hard to stay calm. "I've seen a lot," he said. "You kind of callus over."

He closed his eyes and summoned up his mantra about death, formulated during two months on pain meds in the Camp Lejeune hospital. It was a simple mantra, just the word "Random," over and over, letting himself sink into the last syllable. Good soldier, bad soldier, good guy, bad guy; where the grenade landed was just chance. The opioids imbued the mantra with a gravitas it might otherwise have lacked.

He'd known the pot world was growing rougher. Some people were hiring armed men to guard their grows. A woman grower had been raped and robbed. And CAMP had upped the tension level for everyone. CAMP was the Campaign against Marijuana Planting, an interagency collaborative of pot-loathing cops from around the state who had volunteered for the assignment. It was fantasy camp with live ammo for the cops, who shot dogs, terrorized locals, and were universally feared and despised.

Yosh had bought his red jeep before CAMP showed up. Likewise his Kawasaki ATV and a bunch of French gardening tools he had the hardware store special order for him. Spider thought he was asking for it. But with CAMP on the scene, Yosh restricted his luxury expenditures to Asian rugs and wall hangings. His SOG, down in the basement, was powered by the new Kyocera polysilicon solar cells, so he was off the electric company's grid. There was no legal basis to search his property, he had explained to Spider. He was safe.

"I'm so sorry," Siobhan said. "I know you two were very close."

How close were they? Once Yosh had seemed like an older brother, bold in his vision, wise in the world. In recent years, listening to Yosh brag about his radio tirades and his material acquisitions, Spider had found him borderline tedious.

"I haven't seen much of him, the last few years," Spider said.

He didn't know what else to say. It seemed incongruous to be chatting, with Yosh's body still lying in the road. Who would have killed him? And with a full-on automatic—not the kind of gun you kept propped up in the hall closet.

He thought about the last time he'd seen Yosh, at Bruno's nine months ago. He had said he was growing a lot more, that he was going to see how much Julie Choate could handle and make decisions based on that. Maybe he'd made the wrong decisions.

A police cruiser drove up next to them, and a florid man with a badge leaned out the window. "Ride with us," he said. "We'll get you back here." The florid man said he was the undersheriff. He was accompanied by a deputy, who was obviously stimulated by the situation.

"Yosh Steinmetz," the undersheriff said as he drove. "Friend of yours?"

"Friend of mine," Spider said.

"The better living through vegetables man," the undersheriff said. When his passengers didn't reply, he continued, "Thought he was so smart, with his vegetable van full of pot."

"Got himself a new Jeep now," the deputy said. "Bright red one."

"Red as Hades," the undersheriff said. "Which is where he'll drive it. You a dealer?" he said toward the backseat.

"Excuse me," Siobhan said. "Are we under suspicion here? Aren't there some procedures you want to remember?"

"I wasn't speaking to you, young lady," the undersheriff said, "but I'll take your concern under advisement." The deputy sniggered. "You're not suspects. Not yet anyway. How you doing on that list, Robertson?" he added, addressing the deputy.

"List, sir?"

"The list of people who might want to kill Yosh Steinmetz. I guess it might take a while."

The deputy got in the spirit. "Sir, yes sir. That is an extremely long list. It looks a lot like the phone book."

"You'd put his business partners right at the top. Very volatile business he was in."

"Yes sir, and then there was the show."

"Ha," the undersheriff said. "Bill Ricci! I wouldn't be surprised if we found his business card stuck on the corpse." He laughed at his own joke. "Nah, Ricci's not that stupid. Gotta be someone he shorted or something, bringing an accounting error to his attention."

When they reached the body, the undersheriff turned to Spider and Siobhan and said, "You wait here."

"How are you?" Spider asked Siobhan when they were alone. "I'm sorry you had to go through this."

"I've been sheltered, I guess," she said. "I deal with cases where people are poisoned, but I don't have to inspect the bodies." She thought for a second. "We had a couple little potbellied pigs in Kingman. We gave them names, but we ate them just the same, made jokes. That's as close as I've been."

"Take a deep breath," Spider said. "You're a bit in shock, I think."

She inhaled, breathed out. "I'm in shock," she said. "But still a lawyer. That sheriff…" She shivered in disgust.

"That asshole wasn't all wrong," Spider said. "Yosh did his best to get people mad."

Other cars were pulling up—three police cruisers and a Jeep Cherokee, which disgorged a rumpled man with a jumbo mustache and long graying hair. He wore a shapeless brown corduroy sport coat over a blue work shirt and red necktie and seemed improbably upbeat for a murder scene. He was on first-name terms with the deputies.

The undersheriff returned from the crime scene and conferred with the other police while the man in the sport coat hovered on the outskirts of the circle, openly eavesdropping. One of the deputies peeled off from the group and walked over to Spider and Siobhan in the undersheriff's cruiser.

"Boss man says I should run you back to your car."

The man in the sport coat materialized. He said he was Matt from the *Ukiah Daily Journal*, and a friend of Yosh's. "Really sorry," he said. He still seemed pretty happy to have a scoop. "You guys need a ride to your car? I'll take a couple of photos and give you a lift. Where you staying?"

"We were going to stay with Yosh," Spider said. "I guess we'll drive back to the City." It was a three-hour drive, but he was way too wired to sleep any time soon.

The man drove them back down the gravel road toward Spider's car. "He was something, Yosh," he said.

He didn't elaborate, so Siobhan said, "Something how?"

"Will Rogers never met a man he didn't like," the reporter said. "Yosh was the opposite. But people loved it. The show, I mean. It was like watching a train wreck."

"You were his friend," Spider said.

"Well," the reporter said, "in the broad sense of the term. He liked to fry the paper's butt, and he didn't like all my stories." He thought a moment. "Pretty much none of them, to be honest. But I tried not to take it personally. Looks like someone took it personally, though—with an Uzi or something."

On the drive back to San Francisco, Siobhan asked, "You think there's anything to what the sheriff said? That it's a drug thing?"

"I don't know," Spider said. "It's not impossible, I guess. Or maybe the cops killed him. Yosh really got in their face." Spider had to smile. "He got a bunch of people together, took CAMP to court for civil rights violations, and got a federal judge to ban CAMP helicopters from descending on people's crappers. You should have heard Yosh crow. He did like to rub it in."

"It could have been a deal gone bad," Siobhan said. "You can't rule that out."

"Anything's possible."

They drove in silence for a long time, and then Siobhan said, "The deputy and the reporter, they both said everyone hated him. Really?"

"He did tear a lot of people a new one. Most took it in stride, I think. Yosh being Yosh. But yeah, he wasn't Mr. Congeniality."

By the time they got to Bernal Hill, it was six in the morning. Siobhan showered and was asleep before Spider returned from his own shower to fall asleep beside her.

At noon, they made love—differently, with less abandon, very simply, as if to put on record the fact that they were still alive and with each other again after the passage of considerable time. It seemed incongruous to enjoy themselves too much the day after Yosh was killed, but their bodies had a logic of their own and eventually prevailed.

Chapter 9

San Francisco, Monday, June 17

JULIE CHOATE DROVE TOO FAST ON BROADWAY, ON the short drive home to Pacific Heights from North Beach. A cop pulled her over, but when he saw that she was in a wheelchair in her specially rigged van, and a looker to boot, he let her off with a warning. She was hugely upset. There'd been Yosh's death on Saturday night, and with it the demise of her income. She had run through her trust fund, in no small part as a result of donations to the Black Panthers while they were under attack by Nixon's COINTELPRO. She still lived well, in the retrofitted garage apartment of a Pacific Heights Victorian in which she housed itinerant radicals for months on end. But it was her family's mansion, not hers.

The second blow had been delivered at the humiliating blind date she had just endured. MS had not eliminated her sex drive. Sometimes, she had no interest in what had previously been her favorite pastime, but other times she felt like the same old Julie. There had been men in her life since her illness came on, but not for months. So she had been looking forward to the date that friends had set up with the alternative press editor. She was beautiful and she knew it. As she had dressed, she imagined being in the arms of the editor, a large bald man, not her type exactly, but robust and acceptable.

He hadn't even known it was a date! He looked at her as if she were already dead and gave no hint of viewing her as a sexually interested woman. All he wanted to talk about was the State of the Movement. Fuck the movement, she thought, she had a right to a life. Which is when the cop's revolving red light appeared in her rear view mirror.

After the cop let her go, Julie took some deep breaths and drove home. In her driveway, she pushed the button that sequentially activated the exit ramp of her van, opened the van door and turned her chair sideways toward the exit. She rolled through the front door of her apartment and had just put on the teakettle when the door chime rang.

She rolled to the door and looked through the peephole. A handsome, small Latin man she didn't know was standing there politely, an ingratiating smile on his face. "Senorita Hoolie," he said. "I am Esteban."

She didn't feel much like a senorita. "Hello, Esteban," Julie said from her side of the door "What can I do for you?" She assumed he was looking for work.

"I pay my respects," Esteban said. "For the loss of your partner. I knew him well. May I come in?"

Seated on the edge of the chair she'd motioned him toward, Esteban stared at his hands, his head bowed. "What a tragedy," he said.

Julie's business relationship with Yosh was not broadcast from the rooftops. Esteban's air of familiarity was unsettling. "How did you know Yosh?"

The man smiled. He had good teeth. "We, you and I, are in the same, how you say, the same boat…"

This guy knew about her, and she didn't know about him. "And he happened to mention me?"

"Well, he must do so. To explain why he couldn't meet our full order. Once he explained, of course we understood."

Julie felt very tired. She'd known Yosh was growing more than she could move, but she hadn't known how he'd solved the problem. Not that it was her business how much Yosh grew and how he distributed it. She felt like she'd caught a dead lover stepping out. "What can I do for you, Esteban?" she said again.

"No," Esteban said. "The question is, what can we do for each other?"

Esteban proceeded to explain his idea. She would move into Yosh's house, secure the premises, keep the operation in motion. Then, before too long, they would arrange a different, more permanent solution for keeping the pipeline intact. A handyman would be at her disposal for any tasks that required him.

"I don't know anything about growing," Julie said. "And as you can see, I'm not really configured for manual labor. Why don't you do it yourself?"

"Medellin man moves into dead drug dealer's house?" Esteban said. "Maybe not such a good look.

"I have a feeling," he added, "that if you are there, the rest will fall into place."

She continued to look dubious.

"You are very busy, we know that," Esteban said. "You fight all the time for the people, we admire that. We would make a good contribution to you. Ten thousand dollars for one month. Five now, five at the end of the month. Does that sound fair?"

He reached into his pocket and took out a stack of hundred-dollar bills. "They are real," he said. "You can take them to the bank to be sure before you decide."

She could live for six months on that. Put a sustainability plan together. "Okay," she said. "I'll give it a month. Assuming the bank takes these."

"One month," Esteban agreed. "Can you start right away?"

"Is the house open?"

"I will see to it," Esteban said. He wrote a phone number on the pad next to the phone. "My pager," he said. "I'll call you right back. Any time." He seemed ready to go.

"Wait," Julie said, "Before you go. What do you know about all this?"

Esteban looked blank. "All what?" he said.

"Our mutual friend. Our mutual golden goose shot full of holes."

"Ah," Esteban said. "Of course. I am being very not sensitive. Very sad. Heartbreaking." He shook his head.

"Yes, of course," Julie said. "What's your theory?" Esteban did his blank look again. "Who did it?"

"Ah," he said. "My theory." He screwed his face into thinking mode. "My theory is..." He paused dramatically. "Could be anybody! The man had *muchos enemigos*."

"Were you his *enemigo*?" Julie said.

Esteban laughed. "He was, like you say, golden goose. Who would be enemigo with golden goose?" He did his thoughtful look again. "Maybe another goose. A jealous goose, eh?"

"Yeah," Julie said. "I guess."

Chapter 10

Ukiah, Tuesday, June 18

CAL ALBRIGHT USUALLY ENJOYED HEARING BAYOU PLAY GUITAR and sing. He sounded just like Hank Williams, nasal and lonesome.

Bayou was a wiry man with a lustrous, full red beard, which he compared to Samson's locks and vowed never to shave until white people could live freely in their native land. He was singing about Simon Houston, who had executed a couple of nosy game wardens and then avoided capture in the recesses of the Gorge River in Bedford Forrest County, not all that far from Reverend Footman's Ararat compound. It took the cops almost two years to run him down and put him away, and then he escaped and it took them another year to find him.

It was a terrific song, but Cal wasn't in a musical mood. It was Monday evening, their third day in the woods after taking down the Brink's truck. It had been Cal's plan to camp out while the dragnet exhausted itself. Now they would have to wait even longer, after Ernie had shot the radio guy on Saturday. Ernie still hadn't shown. Cal was losing patience with Ernie.

The men had spent the first day basking in euphoria. Three million three hundred thousand—three times what they had expected. Money for weapons, for computer equipment, for security technology. Money to resettle white people in the bastion.

Money, too, for the men who had made it possible. This had never been fully discussed. They were all doing it for the cause, but it was understood that the men would be rewarded. Cal told the men he was working on a disposition plan and would share it as soon as it was ready.

With his usual foresight, Cal had planned ahead to occupy the men's time in the woods. He gave each man a copy of a book called *The Road Back*, a practical treatise on urban guerrilla warfare. Each of the warriors was assigned to lead a topic: how to create and maintain a revolutionary organization, how to gather intelligence, how to communicate when all hell cut loose, how to organize a modern underground railway. Cal led the session on biological and chemical warfare, instructing the men how to bring a city to a dead stop by igniting gas in the sewer system.

The amount of the haul had raised the men's expectations, Cal could see that. Every chance he got, he reminded the guys that what differentiated them from common thieves was that they were stealing for a purpose, to provide a future for white children. That's where Ernie would have come in useful, by agreeing with everything Cal said and supplying a bible verse to ice the cake.

The killing had chased the Brink's holdup out of the headlines of the *Daily Journal,* which Cal had picked up in front of McDonald's that morning, cautiously reconnoitering, looking for signs of roadblocks or other police presence. He assumed these would only increase with the murder on top of the holdup. What in the name of Yah was Ernie thinking?

He wasn't thinking at all, Cal thought. That was the problem.

Somewhere in the sage tonight the wind calls out his name.
Ai, ai, ai

As Bayou keened the last "ai," Utah came to Cal's side. "Call 'em together, Cal, like we talked about. We have to stay clear in our minds and our spirits."

Cal shouted out, "Gather round, kinsmen. Utah's got a few words to share with us."

Cal edged closer to the table, something to lean against while Utah communed with Yah, with Whom he was on familiar terms. Everyone bowed their heads and shifted their feet, trying to find comfortable ways to stand, since they knew Utah could go on for a spell once he and Yah got a good conversation going.

Utah looked like a short, square-bearded Old Testament prophet. "Yah is a refuge and a fortress," he began in his incongruous reedy voice. He embroidered on this theme for five minutes and then rounded into the home stretch. "Surely, Yah will deliver you from the snare of the fowler and the noisome pestilence. He shall cover thee with His feathers and under His wings shall thou trust. Thou shall not be afraid of the terror by night, nor of the arrow that flieth by day."

Cal imagined being covered with Yah's feathers. The sound of a car driving too fast on the forest road interrupted his reverie. The other men heard it too. They doused their fire, but the car was upon them. The driver hit the brakes and jumped out. When they saw it was Ernie, the men relaxed their grip on their weapons.

"Scared you, huh?" Ernie said. "Don't shoot." He advanced to the smoldering fire. "Sorry to be late," Ernie said. "I had a terrible scare with my little girl. I'm still shaking a bit. Got a beer handy?"

Thor, whose little girl had asthma, brought Ernie a beer. "What happened, partner?"

"She just kinda turned blue," Ernie said. "She's never had no asthma or nothing, but all of a sudden, we look at her and she's gasping for air and her color's changing."

"To blue," Cal said.

"That's right," Ernie said.

"So you went to the hospital," Cal said.

"Well, maybe we should have, but I don't trust the Jew doctors. We just sat there with her all night and most of the day, with cold compresses and hot water bottles, and I don't know what all. And around six she opened her eyes and said, 'Mom and Dad, I have been to the most beautiful place.' And she was back to normal."

"Sometimes really sick people cross over and then cross back," Thor said. "That means they're blessed."

"Lord, I sure hope so," Ernie said. "We've had us a terrible fright."

"Let me buy you another beer, Ernie," Cal said, and propelled him by the elbow to the cooler. "You didn't happen to run any little errands while your girl was crossing over, did you?" When Ernie looked blank, Cal said, "I mean the radio Jew that got shot up."

"I heard on the TV about that. The Lord smites His foes, I'd say."

"The Lord needed some help on this one," Cal said. "That wouldn't have been you helping Him out, was it?"

"You told me to hold off!"

"You're not having fun with me, Ernie?"

"What are you talking about?"

"Okay, Ernie," Cal said, and walked back to the fire

The fire was just embers, and the men around it had fallen silent. Cal told them it was time for his disposition report and the men looked up eagerly. "Article Five," he began, "of our compact. 'We are not thieves, but transferrers of wealth, from the agents of the ZOG to the agents of Aryan Freedom.' Let's all sit with that for a minute."

They sat with it, and then Cal read a list of all the things the money would buy for the Movement. After a long list of hardware, he said, "Five thousand dollars per family resettlement allowance to build the bastion."

There was some mumbling, and Cal said, "Now I'm going to talk about what's coming back to each of us. I've given this a lot of thought and tried to be guided by our principles. But before I talk numbers, I want to talk attitude. The biggest mistake you can make is to start spending fast. Let's say you want to upgrade your vehicle. Fair enough. But for the love of Pete, don't go and plunk a big wad on a bright new chariot, which will draw the attention of the ZOG. Get a six hundred dollar jalopy with a sound motor. Then cherry it out. Spend five hundred on a paint job and three hundred on tires and four hundred on the interior, and the ZOG will be none the wiser. Do you see what I'm saying?"

"Thanks for the home ec lesson," Thor said. "You can move along."

Cal didn't appreciate his tone. Thor was the one most likely to kick up a ruckus. Cal announced that each man who participated would get ten thousand dollars of hazard pay for the Brink's takedown, and was henceforward on retainer for future actions at the rate of two thousand a month.

There was a moment of stunned silence, and then a half-dozen men started talking at once. Thor said, "Screw that, Cal. I got a kid with bad asthma and a buttload of bills. I figure I might get a little more for the risk I took."

Bayou said, "I get ten grand for risking life in prison, and you're paying folks five to just move here? Are you kidding me?"

"Remember!" Cal thundered. "We are race patriots not two-bit common thieves."

Thor took umbrage at this, and the men faced off chest to chest. Bayou joined in, informing Cal he was a tinpot dictator, no better than what they were fighting against.

Utah yelled, "I beseech thee, Yah," in a voice so loud and commanding and so unlike his usual quaver that everyone stopped in amazement. Utah then enjoined their Creator to banish divisions and remind them of their common purpose on behalf of their race.

When Utah was done, everyone got a grip. Cal agreed to double the hazard allotment to twenty thousand and the monthly stipend to four grand. Thor was happy about that and Bayou took back what he had said about Cal being no better than the ZOG.

Cal said he had another target in mind, and to keep logging onto LibertyNet, where more information would soon be shared.

Cal knew that he was the only guy there who owned a computer; the others had to go to the public library to log on. "I know it's a stretch for some of you," he said. "But stick with it, please. It's a big weapon for us if we're smart about using it." Cal loved LibertyNet. Once you entered your password, you could type messages back and forth as well as read Pastor Jack Yardley's column "This I Believe," and news about the Posse Comitatus, the National Alliance, the Sagebrush Rebellion, the Covenant, the Sword, and the Arm of the Lord, and all the Klan chapters. You felt a part of something very big.

On LibertyNet, everyone used pseudonyms, and you had to pass a test to get onto the site, but that wasn't secure enough for Cal. He had designed a code for his warriors. If someone entered a phone number, you added one to the first digit, subtracted two from the second, added three to the third, and so on, to get the real number. And if you needed to mention someone by name, or mention a place name, you did the same thing with the letters. It was a pain in the neck, but Cal insisted.

•••

ERNIE POKED THE EMBERS WITH HIS MARSHMALLOW STICK. He felt all churned up inside. First, the exhilaration of listening to the radio in the Brink's office. Then there was the fond evening with Suzie, and then the ordeal of the camping trip. Telling the guys about it, Ernie almost convinced himself that Jen had been at death's door, and not just hysterical from getting bitten by red ants and running around in a panic in the cold night air.

Then there was showing up at the rendezvous and Cal acting like a hostile stranger. People often had a way of letting him down. He could see Cal was sure he had shot Steinmetz. Maybe he shouldn't have corrected him, Ernie thought. He found it hard to think straight. After being up all night Saturday, Ernie had slept most of Sunday and then he'd gone to work as usual on Monday. Then he'd rushed to the forest rendezvous. What the hell was Cal's beef?

He was on his fifth beer now. It didn't taste nearly as good as the first four. He followed the other men in unrolling their sleeping bags. He thought about the Jew radio guy getting what was coming to him, and wondered who had finally had enough of the Jew's smart mouth. He wished he *had* done it. It was probably a drug deal gone bad, Ernie thought, and then he had another idea. Why not collect Ricci's reward? Ernie rechecked his logic. If no one else claimed the payoff, why shouldn't they?

Ernie tried to imagine how much it would be, coming from a big man like Ricci. Cal would want a cut, of course. Fifty-fifty, Ernie thought—that sounded about right. He was the one who had done the work, after all.

At breakfast, Ernie went up to Cal and said, "I told you a whopper. I did kill that son of Satan."

"Tell me how it went down," Cal said.

"I waited down his road and blocked his way, and when he got out, pow."

"With the Ingram?"

"Yeah."

"Which was to be used only in an emergency."

"Shoot, I considered it an emergency, okay? I bet Mr. R. would consider it an emergency. So stop acting like you're God almighty."

"Don't bandy Yah's name," Cal said angrily and stalked off.

In the morning, the men removed all traces of themselves from the camp. They would use their own cars for the journeys to their respective homes, stowing the getaway vans deep in the woods. They were eager to get going, but Cal called them all together and bade them stand in a circle, cross their arms in front of them, and clasp their neighbors' hands. Cal called it the Aryan knot.

"My brothers," Cal said, and the men repeated his words phrase by phrase. "Let us swear upon our sires' graves, our unborn children, and God's throne.

"Let us be His battle ax and weapons of war.

"We declare ourselves in unrelenting union with each other, without fear of foe or death.

"We hereby invoke the blood covenant."

Chapter 11

"WHAT I REALLY OUGHT TO DO IS GET the interviews out of the way and then come back down for a long weekend," Siobhan announced to Spider, after they had slept into the afternoon on Monday. She would work out of a Ukiah motel through Thursday, she said.

Spider tried to think up some way they could spend the whole week together, especially since he intended to return to Ukiah himself. But then he thought better of it and agreed with her plan.

Tuesday morning, he saw her off in the garage's loaner Volvo. It was a relief, in a way. He needed some space to think about what happened and about the file cabinet key Yosh had given him nine months before. He hadn't told Siobhan about it. He needed to see what was in the files before he would know what to think.

Wednesday morning, he left early for Ukiah, arriving at Yosh's at eleven. There was a van parked in front of the house. He knocked on the front door. When Julie Choate opened it, they eyed each other in mutual surprise.

She spoke first. "Well, isn't this a coinkidink. Are you house-sitting too? Come on in." She was rattling away as she wheeled around, leading him into the house. "I appointed myself executor, on the assumption Yosh didn't have a will. There are some assets here that wouldn't be appreciated by the bank."

"He didn't have a will?" Spider said.

"Maybe," she said. "And you were in the neighborhood?"

There didn't seem to be any compelling reason to lie to her, so he told Julie about Yosh's rogues' gallery. She followed him into the office, and he unlocked the cabinet. The top drawer was almost full; it looked like there were upwards of fifty file folders. Spider checked the other drawer, which was empty, and then they went back to the dining room and pawed through the folders. Yosh had antagonized multitudes. He took sides on every county squabble. He said those who would remove "The Story of O" from the Willets library needed to get laid, and he led the charge to fire a deputy sheriff who spouted his racist sentiments during a drug bust. Bill Ricci's folder was the thickest. Julie's presence distracted him. What was she really doing there?

"This is going to take some time," Spider finally said. He stacked the folders and hoisted them. "I'll give these a close look later," he said. "Maybe something will jump out."

"Sit down and talk to me," Julie said. "Don't you want to know the real reason I'm here?"

She served them coffee in the breakfast nook. She moved fluidly in her chair, supporting herself on the countertop when she needed to stand, gracefully arranging the Melitta filter, adding coffee and pouring boiling water from an electric kettle, declining Spider's offer to assist.

Julie had a cane attached to the wheelchair, and she used it to get around the living room. She looked spry enough, as if she could even dispense with the cane if she felt like it. Spider wondered how sick she really was. Yosh had said her symptoms came and went.

DANIEL BEN-HORIN

"I am, in a word, destitute," she told Spider, lifting her coffee cup to her lips and smiling brightly. "And that is why I am here. The show must go on. Somehow."

"You're going to grow pot? Here?"

"Yes," she said, and then added, "Not all by myself, of course." He raised his eyebrows, but she changed the topic. "What about you?" she said. "You must be all shook, no?"

Was he all shook? "I'll miss him," Spider said.

"I will too. He and I went way back, to the FSM. And the Panthers after that. We were comrades in struggle. And in bed. Did he tell you about us?"

"We only talked about you eighty percent of the time," Spider said. She smiled, and Spider gave her points for a sense of humor.

"Who killed him, do you think?" Julie said.

"I was going to ask you that," Spider said. "I have no idea. I wasn't part of his business."

"Maybe it had nothing to do with his business. Maybe it was someone who didn't like him, or his politics. It's been known to happen. Like, every day."

"The cops think it was a deal gone bad," Spider said. "Do you know who he dealt with, aside from you?"

"Are you going to read me my rights?" Julie said. "No, I don't know who he dealt with aside from me."

He wondered who was helping her grow pot, but there was an etiquette to such matters. She hadn't volunteered the information, and she obviously wouldn't, now that he'd gotten her dander up.

Julie sat down suddenly on the couch and said, "Whew. I get so tired—just sweeps over me." She sat for a moment and then said, "Would you help me to my chair? I need to go lie down." He wheeled the chair toward her, and she leaned on him and slid into it. "Forgive me for not seeing you out." She wheeled toward the bedroom.

"Good luck with the grow," Spider said. "Watch out for CAMP helicopters."

The forest road was empty as he drove out. His thoughts turned to Siobhan, in Ukiah sopping up the gyppos' stories. He considered surprising her at her motel. He decided against it; he didn't want to seem like a puppy dog following her around. He would talk to her the next night, when she returned from her interviews. He would cook for her, he decided. Roll out the stuffed squid.

Chapter 12

San Francisco, Thursday, June 20, to Sunday, June 23

IN SPIDER'S FIRST YEAR IN SAN FRANCISCO, A lover had served him baked, stuffed squid, touting its aphrodisiacal effects. He had mastered that dish and no other. It was a foolproof female-pleaser. Whether it was the squid itself or the potent effect of a big man moving around a kitchen, the dish had served its purpose on a number of occasions.

Thursday night, after a long drive and a long bath, Siobhan sprawled on Spider's couch while, in the kitchen, Spider peeled the skin off the cephalopods and washed out their body cavities. "This one guy, you should have seen him, he was wrapped head to toe like a mummy," she called out as Spider chopped tentacles. "He said he had to run across a hornets' nest because the winch line broke and the cat was going to roll into a ravine."

"Cats generally land on their feet," Spider said. "They're famous for it." It was like working on her Fiat while she dissected the *Arizona Republic*. He felt as he had back then, that it was something he could get used to.

"Caterpillar," she said. "A tractor."

"Ah," Spider said. "What does that have to do with your lawsuit?"

"Nothing, unfortunately," Siobhan said. "Spider, I don't think there is much of a lawsuit."

"Why not?" Spider said. "Don't you need to do about five or ten years more research?"

"I'm going to have to come up with a different reason to see you," she said. "There's just not enough numerosity to move forward. We could bring an action if they had sprayed a large area, and then a large number of loggers were sent into that area to work and they all had similar secondary exposure to the chemical as a result. But what we have is one small, specific group of people getting directly sprayed on a particular day, and then another specific group getting sprayed on another day, and so on. And I think the foremen knew something in advance but don't want to admit it. The defense would tear us apart. We wouldn't even get certified as a class."

Spider didn't say anything. He felt like she was evading the point. He mixed the tentacles and garlic with ricotta cheese, pine nuts, and raisins.

"They could still bring a bunch of individual cases," Siobhan plowed on. "Through Hymie and Ike. That's what the gyppos call the Jewish personal injury lawyers in Healdsburg."

"Nice," Spider said.

"Oh, they're racist and anti-Semitic and misogynistic and environmentally vicious and generally wacko. Entertaining, though."

"Still kind of pond scum."

"Everyone deserves to be represented."

To Spider, it didn't sound like her heart was in it. He stuffed the mixture he'd concocted into the squids' excavated carcasses, arranged the little blimps in a baking dish and put the dish in the oven.

He liked how she ate. When she enjoyed something, she put it away. "I can't wait to see what you cook tomorrow night," she said.

"That's it," he said. "That's my dish."

"That's it? You have one dish and it's stuffed squid?"

"It never fails," he said. "After that, they cook."

•••

THE SUBJECT OF HIS VISIT TO YOSH'S FILE cabinet managed not to come up after the squid. The next morning, she needed to spend the day in the UC Berkeley law library. Spider said he would play basketball with his old pal Ohanian, and she could drop by the gym whenever she was ready and they'd go out and eat together. "I've known Ben about twelve hours longer than I knew Yosh," Spider told her.

They played at a Y on the edge of the Tenderloin. It was a full-court game of players who'd suited up for their high schools or even played some in college. Siobhan showed up as the last game began; she was the only spectator. Spider felt good as fuck-all to be the one she was watching. He blocked a shot, and instead of handing the ball off to a guard, he dribbled the length of the court, stopped as if to pass, and then accelerated past the startled defender directly to the basket. He glanced over at her, but she was writing in a notebook.

"So what's with you and Mr. Mean?" Ohanian asked Siobhan after the game.

"He's complimenting my rebounding," Spider said, "without which he might spend two hours here and never touch the ball."

"I'm an artist," Ohanian said. "I leave the heavy work to the common folk."

"Are you an artist?" Siobhan said.

"Yes, in a parallel universe. In this one, I am an aide and dogsbody for one of our state senators."

"Ben is too modest," Spider said. "He's the Svengali who pulls the strings."

"Really?" Siobhan said. "I think about switching jobs sometimes. I'd like to work for someone with vision—and passion. It would beat what I'm doing now. Is your boss full of vision and passion?"

"He's a pusillanimous wimp," Ohanian said, "who started out in the Free Speech Movement and ended up in the Free Money Movement. Let's go drink."

They settled on Brennan on the Moor, an Irish bar in the inner Richmond with good hamburgers. THREE WOMEN SOUGHT FOR SEXUAL ASSAULT screamed the banner on the TV above the bar. The women, up in the Sierra gold country, were on the lam for pistol-whipping two men and forcing them to fellate each other. Authorities claimed it was part of a drug deal gone sour.

"Crime wave," Spider said.

"Not by my standards," Siobhan said.

A table got loud. It was full of Muni bus drivers in their khaki berets and vests festooned with Croix de Candlestick pins, emblems of enduring an extra-inning night game at subarctic Candlestick Park. A middle-aged black woman toasted a sallow, bespectacled young man wearing the map of Ireland on his face. Spider deduced this was the honoree, though he looked more like a defendant.

"Happy birthday to our dispatcher," the woman said, "who does his job and mostly lets us do ours." There was a noisy clinking together of beer mugs and shot glasses.

"I am a ruined man," the sallow fellow said. "Aren't at least six of you working tonight? And me watching you get sloshed."

Spider went to the bar to order their burgers and grab a pitcher of Anchor Steam.

"So, tell, what wind blew you here?" Ohanian asked Siobhan, twirling his mustache.

"We knew each other in Arizona years ago."

"Ten," Spider said, returning with the beer. "But she dumped me."

"Well," Siobhan said. "Not exactly."

"And now she has picked you back up," Ohanian said. "I love happy endings. Are you having a blast here?"

"Well," she said.

"My friend got shot and killed, up in Ukiah," Spider said. "But I'm glad she's here."

"Oh, right," Ohanian said. "I forgot you knew him. He was on my boss's shit list, so I think well of him. Who did it?"

"They don't know," Spider said. "The sheriff said it was a pot thing, but I don't think he knows that for sure. Yosh pissed a lot of people off."

"He pissed off Bill Ricci," Ohanian said. "And when Bill is pissed, my guy holds the pot. My guy told Ricci to sue for libel."

"Truth is a defense. Was it true?" Siobhan asked.

"Probably," Ohanian laughed. "Ricci is not a nice man."

"I know that," Siobhan said. "He's why I'm here." She explained about Garlon and the gyppos.

They were on their second pitcher of Anchor and almost done with the burgers. The pale Muni dispatcher wandered over to the jukebox and sang along with his selection. It was something about young Roddy McCorley marching to his death on the Bridge of Toome.

"So," Spider said, "I have some new info." He told them about the files now residing in his car trunk. "His private enemies list. Maybe fifty, sixty different leads."

"You say they're in your trunk?" Siobhan said.

For the next two hours, they drank and passed the folders around. The Muni party dissipated. The files adding up to a maddening collage. What was one to make, for example, of Yosh's handwritten notes about a rapist who phoned in after each attack? There were notes of five calls and no record of any arrest.

Or the Spanish-language newspaper clippings from a Bogota paper. Spider spoke enough Spanish to piece out the text, though the photos told the story clearly enough. Four cousins had been executed, the youngest, nine. The killers cut off their arms and legs and left them to bleed to death. They pinned a note to the kid— "This is what happens to the families of snitches."

"I have an idea," Siobhan said. She told them about a private investigators forum on her Grapevine computer network. "They'll eat this up," Siobhan said. "They live for stuff like this."

Ohanian grinned broadly and exclaimed, "I'm *DrO*! What's your pseud?"

"Shut up!" Siobhan said. "I love your posts. I'm *calamityjane*." Ohanian liked Siobhan's idea of recruiting the P.I. Forum members to comb the material and identify threats.

"I don't know," Spider said. "They won't have much to work with." He felt like he'd fallen down a rabbit hole.

"What have we got to lose?" Siobhan said. "It beats just sitting around waiting for that creepy cop to do something." She would reach out to the forum manager the very next day, when she wasn't tipsy, she said.

That night, Spider awoke in a fetal position, venting great racking sobs. Siobhan tried to hold him, but it did little to dampen the explosion. After a while, he laid on his back breathing spasmodically. She went into the kitchen and brought back a damp towel for his forehead. Spider's breath returned to regular intervals.

"I'm sorry," he said. "I have no idea what just happened. I had a dream." He paused, trying to summon it again. Fragments chased each other across his brain, but he couldn't piece them together. There had been bodies, lots of them, he could remember that much. "Death," he finally said. "I thought I could handle it, but I was wrong."

"Are you okay?" Siobhan said. He was very pale.

"I am now, I think," he said.

•••

THEY SPENT SATURDAY HIKING DRAKES ESTERO IN POINT Reyes, admiring the elk and blue herons. He told her about Julie Choate being at Yosh's house and what he knew about her. There wasn't much to say after a while. Her departure hung over them like the day's ocean fog, which never quite lifted.

Sunday morning, the sun rose bright behind the Oakland hills. The Bay shimmered on their left as they drove south on 101 to the airport. The dilapidated projects of Potrero Hill, Bayview, and Hunters Point sparkled. It was as if the elements were teaming up to help Spider make the case for San Francisco.

"What happens now?" he said.

"That's what I love about you," she said. "You're so aggressive."

"What happens now!" Spider said in an aggressive voice.

She laughed. "What Is To Be Done!"

"Right."

"It's the name of a book, the Leninist bible. Lenin wrote it when things were at a crossroads."

"Just like us."

"Are there Citroëns in New York?"

"They're everywhere. It's a cult."

"So, uh, do you see where I'm going with this? I could slow it down, if you like."

"Uh huh," Spider said. It was true that Citroën owners obsessed over their cars, but his success in San Francisco was a function of time and place and meeting Yosh. It wouldn't be nearly that simple in New York. He'd have to start as a mechanic, build a following. It wouldn't be half as much fun as running The New People's Garage.

"What if I visit you?" Spider said. "I've never been."

"Thataboy," she said. "I can't wait to show you Avenue A." She sounded giddy in a way that Spider found hard to read. He didn't want to dance around with her.

"Look," he said. "I tried out letting you get away, and that didn't work out so great for me. Are we together or not?"

"Like pinned?" she said. "Going steady?" He didn't answer. "I'd like that, I think."

"Okay," he said. "I'll fly out Thursday." She looked surprised, but when Spider decided to do something, he didn't turn it over in his mind a hundred times. "Too soon?" he asked.

She mulled the concept of Spider in New York. "No," she said. "More like overdue."

"Okay," he said, "Let me know if you change your mind." He thought a second and said, "Don't."

Driving home, clouds covered the sun and the East Bay looked drab and normal. Tankers dotted the bay, patches of black, red and yellow. New York! He thought. He had tried to avoid it, like Disneyland and Las Vegas. He didn't feel a world of confidence, but he was willing to give it a try.

Chapter 13

New York, Sunday, June 23, to Sunday, June 30

MEL WAS ON TOP OF THE WORLD. THE Sunday *New York Times* had just splashed the Grapevine over the front page of their *Trends* section. They called Mel a "precocious programmer" and a "visionary" and gave respectful space to his anarcho-Marxist views.

The Grapevine had grown to eight thousand users across the country, and while it was obvious that communicating via computer could never replace face-to-face interaction, no one could deny that something interesting was afoot. Grapevine users paid whatever they felt like for the privilege of using the system. Mel reminded the *Times* reporter that property was theft and said the Grapevine would never refuse its service to someone who couldn't pay.

He could get used to being in the *Times*. Three months before, the paper had named him to its list of "twenty people who will determine the fate of the City's housing stock." He was right next to the nun who ran the Diocese's low-income renters' program. The *Times* said the City's squatter movement was the most vibrant of its kind worldwide and that much of the credit was owed to the "indefatigable and irrepressible" founder of Elephant House.

The City became for him a smorgasbord of public events, panel discussions, and tête-a-têtes with influential people. The whirlpool of political conviviality had left less time for hanging out at the squat, or scavenging Village dumpsters, or visiting his girlfriend, especially once she had tired of being arm candy at events and dinners.

"You Mel?" asked the man who materialized at the door of his Elephant House office. He wore a leather vest over a wifebeater, which didn't quite cover a roll of flesh that jiggled on his studded belt.

"Me Mel," Mel agreed.

The man looked around the office, and then went back in the hallway and looked around there. "Nice," he said, when he entered again. "And you don't pay a cent of rent." He shook his head in amazement. "Too fucking much."

"You are?" Mel said.

"Hey, sorry, man, call me Tramp," the man said. "I'm an Adder. Maybe you heard about us?"

Everyone in Loisaida had heard about the Adders. They were a Hell's Angels offshoot that made a hobby of beating the crap out of crack dealers. Was extremism in the extirpation of vice a virtue? It was the springtime of Bernie Goetz, the white subway vigilante who had gunned down four black muggers (his story) or panhandlers (their story). People were divided on the subject. In any case, crack dealers were not cherished as neighborhood assets, and the Adders received considerable local approbation.

"We got a clubhouse on Grand, near the river," Tramp continued. "Landlord don't do shit, so we stopped sending him money. We got any rights here? I asked around and people said Mel's the man."

"When did he stop making repairs, the landlord?" Mel asked.

"About three years ago," Tramp said. "Not since he came over once on account of the plumbing being stopped up, and one of the boys helped him see the problem close up. Shit, we told him it was all in fun and wouldn't happen again, but he won't do nothing ever since."

"Does he threaten you?"

"Does *he* threaten *us*?" Tramp asked incredulously.

"With eviction, I mean."

"He's not that dumb," Tramp said. "I mean, we know where he lives."

"Have you improved the premises?"

"Hell yeah," Tramp said. "We put in a big color TV and we got a nice propane barbecue right out front."

"Right," Mel said. "If I were you, I'd sit tight for seven more years and then file for adverse possession."

"That's it?" Tramp said. "Just sit tight? Don't need to mess with no lawyers or nothing?"

"Not unless he files an eviction notice. But like you said."

"We know where he lives."

"Exactly." Mel felt tough, conspiring with the Adder. It would be handy, Mel thought, to develop a working relationship with people who inspired fear in landlords.

Tramp produced a substantial spliff and invited Mel to share it. "How much I owe you for the legal advice?" he said. "Adders always pay their debts."

It struck Mel as an incongruous claim, given their conversation, but he kept the thought to himself. He was feeling good with his new friend. He was feeling good in general.

"Don't worry about it," he said. "We're all in this together."

Mel's euphoric state lasted four days, until Friday morning, when Nestor came in and said, "Girlfriend's back."

Nestor, Mel's factotum, had lived at Elephant House since its inception three years before and made a special point of being informed about all Loisaida matters that might concern Mel. He had told Mel a week ago that Siobhan was apparently not around.

Siobhan hadn't mentioned any trips, but then again, they didn't talk much. Now she was back. He thought about his schedule and decided that over the weekend he would see if Siobhan were up for a visit.

"She's not alone," Nestor added portentously. Mel looked at him.

"A fella," Nestor said. "I saw them snuggling up in the Thai place on Avenue B. I watched them walk back to her house later, hands all over each other."

Mel felt sucker-punched. If Siobhan wanted more than he had been offering her, all she had to do was say something. "Bitch," he said.

"You got that right," Nestor said.

•••

NEW YORK WASN'T NEARLY AS AWFUL AS SPIDER had feared. Siobhan met him at the airport. They took a bus and then a subway and then walked five blocks to a Thai restaurant, where they dined behind iron window bars wrought in dragon shapes. He'd eaten Thai before, but this tasted more real somehow. Had a sharper edge. Walking to her place, they enjoyed a long embrace until she pointed out he was pressing her against a large garbage bag.

Spider liked the sheer mass and texture of the crowds, below and above ground, extracting the last of the spring weather. He liked the Latin way Siobhan pronounced her boisterous neighborhood.

On Friday, while Siobhan was at her office, he walked over to the Village and watched the famous full-court game in the Cage on West Fourth above the subway exit. Maybe just two years ago, he would have worn his sneakers, tried to get in a game. But the elbows under the rim had started to hurt more. He watched the guys pounding and trash talking and taking hard fouls, and didn't aspire to be among them.

It was called the Cage because it was half the size of a normal court and encased in a twenty-foot high metal fence around which spectators clustered, as if they were trying to get into jail. There was no out-of-bounds in the Cage game. The ball bounced off the fence at random angles, and big bodies flung themselves at the ball, the basket, and each other. All the players were black or Latin.

"You hoop?" The question came from near his left shoulder. He turned and found a small, bespectacled black man wearing a duffle coat and a fedora, like it was late autumn instead of early summer.

"Not like this," Spider said.

"You big enough."

"I'm not big on pain."

"You soft. Where you from? I bet you from California."

Spider laughed. "Guilty. San Francisco. You're right, we don't like pain out there. Do you like pain?"

"I'll ask the questions. My name is Nestor. Nestor Johnson. What is yours?"

"Spider Lacey."

"All right. Now we are getting somewhere. Why you here? Standing here right now?"

"I'm visiting someone and I like hoops. Guys back home told me to check out this game."

"Okay," the little man said, as if he had established something important. "And what you do when you're not visiting someone and liking hoops?"

"I work on cars."

"In San Francisco!" he yelled as if he had caught Spider in a contradiction. Spider turned his attention back to the game.

"You bubblegum, man. I gonna chew you up and spit you out," one young man said to another, dribbling on the other side of the fence, a foot from Spider.

"I gonna do you like the ho you be," the dribbler riposted, and slashed toward the basket, leading with his elbow.

"Whose cars?" Nestor pressed.

"Anyone's," Spider said. "Bring your car to the New People's Garage and we'll work on it for you."

"For free?"

"I'll give you a special rate."

"Write it down," the man said. "I might learn to drive, get a car, drive it out to San Francisco, just to see the look on your face." He extended Spider a pen and a notebook.

"New People's Garage. We're in the book," Spider said.

•••

It turned out that the P.I. Forum on the Grapevine consisted of a single aspiring P.I. who enjoyed assuming different personas and engaging in coruscating dialogues with himself. Siobhan was disappointed and spent Friday evening poring over Yosh's files. She developed various theories, each more far-fetched than the one before.

"Let's go out," Spider said. "Like normal people. Get a drink somewhere. Observe the simple local folk."

"All right," Siobhan said. "You could pretend to be from out of town and I'm, like, showing you around. It could work. Wait a minute."

She went into the bedroom, where he could hear her making a phone call. He heard her cackle and say, "See you."

She came out after a bit and said, "Let's go, cowpoke." She was wearing pegged pants, a tee with Katharine Hepburn's face on it, and Sperry topsiders. She looked outstanding, in Spider's measured opinion.

8BC was on Eighth between B and C. The proprietors had removed half of the ground floor, exposing the bare earth cellar. People walked and drank and danced on the dirt. The inside walls were covered with graffiti and dozens of inflatable Ronald Reagan dolls and a painting, called *Civilization Teeters*, of Greek women struggling to hold up a temple despite wild wolves nibbling on their feet.

The owners had left the back half of the floor of the building intact, taking out the walls and thus creating an enormous stage eight feet above the audience. A woman on the stage was performing all the parts in King Lear, flinging herself in and out of costumes that floated down from the rafters on cue.

A woman embraced Siobhan. She was put together: big earrings, a silk shirt, very tight jeans with one knee ripped, a bomber jacket and checkerboard Vans. Spider felt a little underdressed, though Siobhan had assured him he looked great in a well-worn white shirt and jeans. "Sets off your nutty beard," she said. "It's perfect."

Siobhan's friend scrutinized Spider. "So this is him, huh?" she said. "Nice body. Does he talk?"

"Spider, this is Isabel, we work together. It appears that I have mentioned you to her. Which I hope I won't regret." She said the last with a dramatic stare at Isabel, who just laughed.

The Lear woman had departed and musical equipment was being brought onstage. "I was glad you called," Isabel said to Siobhan. "After that rant."

The sound system was loudly piping something Latin, and Siobhan was moving her feet. "What are you talking about?" she said. She moved her hip into Spider's.

"How soon they forget," Isabel said. "We don't have to talk about it if you don't want to. I'll just write it off as a bad dose."

Siobhan stopped bumping Spider. "What are you talking about?" she said again. "Make sense, please."

"What you posted," Isabel said. "About your real opinion of the place."

"I did no such thing," Siobhan said.

The two women conferred rapidly in a way that was hard for Spider to follow, but he got the gist. Someone purporting to be Siobhan had called Grapevine users "losers" and "creeps," afraid of the real world, cravenly hiding behind their anonymous handles.

"It's got to be Mel," Isabel said. "Fasten your seat belt, girlfriend."

"Who's Mel?" Spider said.

Siobhan looked at the ground. Isabel grinned sheepishly. "Let's dance, Sasquatch," she said to Spider, pulling him onto the floor.

"She's really into you," she said. "Trust me. Mel was an aberration."

"I'm sorry," Siobhan said when they were back at her apartment later. "I didn't mean to mislead you. He's someone I was finished with."

"How can he do that? Pretend to be you?" Spider said. "Don't you have, like, a password?"

"He started the Grapevine," Siobhan said. "He has root privileges. He can do what he wants."

"Can you talk to him?" Spider said.

"Sure," she said. "I guess that's the next step." She paused and then said, "No time like the present," and went into her bedroom to the phone, leaving the door open.

"Mel, it's Siobhan; we've got to talk."

"Oh, Mel, come off it."

"Relationship? We've hardly seen each other for the last six months. What relationship?"

"Okay, Mel," she said. "Have it your way. I haven't been happy and I haven't been able to talk to you and now it's over. I could have acted better. I didn't plan it this way. Things just happened. Someone got killed, and it brought Spider and me together."

"Mel," she said. Then she winced and hung up.

"Well, that went well," she said to Spider. "Anyway, I've been told, and I expect he's shot his wad."

•••

HUMIDITY DESCENDED ON THE CITY. SPIDER AND SIOBHAN decided to spend his last New York day, Sunday, beating the heat at Coney Island. They left early, but by the time the F train dropped them off, the beach was already full with blankets and boom boxes, squealing infants, and muscular guys throwing footballs to each other amidst it all.

"The wretched refuse of our teeming shore," Siobhan said, surveying the dense mass of humanity between them and the water.

Spider looked at the unbroken sea of blankets and tried to connect the scene to his concept of a beach. Still, the water, when they managed to reach it, was warmer than the Pacific, and the wretched refuse were endearing in their commitment to enjoying the day.

At seven, they started the long ride home on the F. The fans in the subway car rotated halfheartedly. Salty sweat dripped down Spider's forehead. "I'm not big on leaving you here," he said.

"You're worried about Mel?"

"That too," Spider said. "I'm more worried about me. I want to be with you."

She put her arm around him. It was greased with suntan lotion and sweat and slid off his back. "Me too," she said.

The humidity had soared and then the skies had opened up in a welcome summer shower. The subway car filled with damp people and the smell of sweat. At the York Street station in Brooklyn, before the subterranean traverse of the river, a drenched young woman got on. She shouted incoherent sentiments to the other occupants of the car and then proceeded to remove her T-shirt, revealing full breasts in a white bra.

A group of young Puerto Ricans started clapping their hands rhythmically, chanting "Take it off." The other people in the car looked away. The woman seemed disoriented and frightened, as if only just aware of what had happened and how she appeared. She folded her arms over her chest and started to cry.

Spider said, "Hey, stay calm, it's okay," and started moving toward her. One of the chanters, a banty cock, blocked his way. "Not your business, faggot."

The train rumbled to a halt on the tracks. Spider stood where he was. He towered over the little guy, but there were six or seven of them.

The clapping got louder. The banty cock was chest to belt with Spider. The woman huddled in her seat. Everyone else in the car looked straight ahead.

Then the train restarted with a jolt. Both men stumbled. Quickly they were in the Delancey Street station, where Spider and Siobhan got off, while the train filled with people traveling uptown from Chinatown, Little Italy, and Loisaida.

"Oh, Spider," Siobhan said. "I appreciate that you're not a coward, but in New York, you got to be smart sometimes. They weren't going to hurt that girl. But they would have hurt you. People are crazy."

He thought about Bernie Goetz. The people in the subway car who had ignored the men who were goading the woman—was that being smart? If the little guy had charged him, with his pals at his side, what would have been smart behavior on Spider's part? To flee? To take his licks like a man? It had been his experience—

on the basketball court, in Arizona country bars, in Vietnam, and elsewhere—that there were times when backing down just invited more abuse. There were times you had to dig in.

It wasn't something he could easily explain. Instead, he said, "When will I see you again?"

"How about I come out next weekend?" she said.

Spider felt much better.

•••

A LAWYER IN SIOBHAN'S FIRM WAS HAVING AN affair with a film producer. The couple alternated weekends in LA and New York. That had never struck Siobhan as a real relationship, but now, with airfares plummeting and two good incomes, jetting back and forth didn't seem so outlandish. Eventually, of course, if they got that far, they'd have to settle on one coast or the other. But there was no need to rush it.

Spider stuck his head out of the departing cab and said, "I'm glad to get a second bite of the apple." He ran his tongue across his lower lip and leered at her in a way that made her laugh.

When Siobhan turned into her building, who should be strolling by but Nestor. "Miz S," he said. "How come we don't see you no more?"

"Hi Nestor," she said. "I've been busy. Things change."

"Well, we miss you. We your family. Mel, he misses you so much, it's pitiful."

"I think he's angry with me," Siobhan said. "In fact, I know he is."

"Angry?" Nestor said. "Angry? He ain't angry. He heartbroke. You want the man to say, oh, ho hum, she gone, no big deal? You want him to act like he don't care?"

It seemed odd to be arguing with Mel's proxy. "I'd like to be friends with him, Nestor," she said. "I'd like to come visit you all. It's just not the right time now."

"We your family," Nestor said again. "You don't turn your back on your family."

"I'll see you around," she said.

She unlocked the door to the building, walked up the three flights, and started unlocking the sequence of deadbolts on her front door. Her neighbor, the defiantly still-rent-controlled Mrs. Baumgartner, opened her door and stuck her head out.

"Nice fella, your fella," she said. "Your new fella, I mean. The other one I didn't care for."

Siobhan was fascinated that Mrs. Baumgartner had formed opinions of her lovers. "I like the new one better too," she said, getting the last lock to click. "You'll see him again."

"You're not getting any younger," Mrs. Baumgartner said, "but who is."

It was 10:00 p.m., and Siobhan had every intention of reviewing a brief. She settled herself with a glass of wine, which she managed to put back on the coffee table before her eyes slammed shut. She startled awake in the blackness of 4:00 a.m. and found the switch to the table lamp.

Loisaida was rarely so quiet. She decided to catch up on work. First, though, a cup of coffee and the Grapevine.

She entered her username, *calamityjane*, and her password. The welcome screen formed and then immediately exploded, the ASCII letters dancing all around and then coalescing as a sad face filling the screen.

The face dissolved and reformed into the words I'M SORRY. Which dissolved into the words I LOVE YOU. Her usual welcome screen returned.

She was wide awake now. She threw out her untouched coffee and made a cup of chamomile tea instead. This was going to be a lot more complicated than she had anticipated.

Chapter 14

Ukiah, Thursday, June 27

"YOU RUN ACROSS A LOT OF AUTOMATIC WEAPONRY up here, shootings with automatics, that kind of thing? Pretty par for the course?" the Secret Service agent asked the Mendocino County sheriff, Bart "Hopalong" Cassidy, who was warily enduring his first-ever encounter with the US Secret Service.

"Well," the sheriff said, "not par for the course, no. I mean, we run across everything, but as a typical thing, automatics, no."

"Ever?" the agent said. "Is this a new one for you?"

The agent, whose name was Alex Schollmeyer, did not suffer fools gladly, especially now that his luck had finally turned and he was on the track of something that could jump-start his stalling career.

"Dang it," the sheriff said. "You're right. It is a first." The agent stared at him.

"You think that it's an automatic, uh, tells us something?" the sheriff asked.

Schollmeyer ignored his question. "Your investigator who responded to the call," he looked at his notebook. "Your undersheriff, to be exact, told the media that the crime was likely to be related to the sale of marijuana. Is that your assessment as well, and, if so, on what basis?"

"Well," the sheriff said. "It's one possibility. The victim was a significant grower."

"Among many up here, as I understand it," Schollmeyer said. "But the others don't seem to get shot up with an Ingram Mac-10."

"Which fits your hypothesis," the sheriff said agreeably, wishing he knew what an Ingram Mac-10 was.

"So I'm curious," the agent said. "Do you have any knowledge of the victim interacting with individuals engaged in white supremacy, racism, Nazism, Aryanism, Christian Identity, any of those things?"

"You're kidding," the sheriff said.

Schollmeyer stared at him some more.

"Well, first of all, I'm not sure I know what exactly all those labels mean. But do you have any idea who this guy was? He had more enemies than…" He searched for a comparison. "Genghis Khan. Hitler. He made lots of enemies with his damn show. Put me on the list. But I didn't shoot him."

"That's reassuring," Schollmeyer said. "So he had a lot of enemies, you have no leads, and maybe you're not certain this is a pot-related crime? Here's my card. Let me know if anything comes up you think I should know."

Twelve days had already passed since the murder; it had taken that long for the murder weapon to be identified from ballistics tests and for someone to remember the all points that Schollmeyer had put out on Ingrams. Schollmeyer had flown out from DC immediately upon hearing about the murder weapon, which tied the killing to his current investigation, upon which he was betting his future.

Schollmeyer's twenty years in the Service had been frustratingly devoid of opportunities to shine. When he was on a protection mission, it was just a lot of standing around. When he was on an investigation mission, someone else ended up with the credit.

He'd traced a guy passing twenties in malls from Lewiston, Maine, to Las Cruces, New Mexico. The twenties all had the same tiny defect, which only Schollmeyer had snagged. On the back of the bill, there was a green curl in the sky above the White House and below the letter "T" in "UNITED."

They had interviewed clerks who'd accepted the bills and developed an artist's composite of the passer, which they circulated in fifty states. They finally ran the guy down in Omaha. Trying to find his printing press, they found a storage locker of female body parts instead. The FBI grabbed the case, and Schollmeyer was assigned to some bad tens that had shown up in Providence.

This case was different. Schollmeyer had been recruited by an FBI agent named Foster to the theory that there was a national white supremacist conspiracy, modeled after the novel *The Turner Diaries* and with the same goal as Earl Turner: the establishment of a separate white nation on American territory. Their means, too, were the same as Turner's: robberies, counterfeiting, assassinations, and sabotage of public facilities, aimed at sparking a socially cathartic race war.

A year ago, Foster had pulled some strings and gotten Schollmeyer assigned to the investigation, based on the counterfeiting angle. Despite his superiors' skepticism, Schollmeyer became consumed with the case. He subscribed to Foster's theory that the future of the nation was at stake, from the far right rather than the terrorist left, whose moldering corpse the leaders of both the FBI and the Service were determined to keep kicking around. He felt as he had in November of 1963, as a junior at the University of Minnesota, when he read about the heroic Secret Service agent who had draped his body over the Kennedys in the midst of the gunfire.

Now, Schollmeyer was convinced that the people he was investigating had killed Steinmetz, who was both Jewish and a rightbaiter who flaunted his opinions. The unusual murder weapon, an Ingram Mac-10 illegally retrofitted as a full automatic, was known to have pride of place in the white supremacists' arsenal. A fully automatic Mac-10 was a foolproof killing machine within twenty yards. It had no other uses.

Agent Schollmeyer had developed a low opinion of local law enforcement over the years, and his recent interview with the Mendocino sheriff was grist for his mill. They would use the murder to roust out the local grower community, searching for the gun and a motive, and would find neither.

Schollmeyer drove his rental car to the public radio station. The station manager ushered him into his office, which was lined with bookcases full of tape recordings. "I knew this wasn't about pot," the manager said. "What can I do for you?"

"How did you know it wasn't about pot?"

"Yosh gave fair weight," the manager said. "That's what I'm told," he added hastily. "You don't believe that CAMP horseshit, do you? People have guns to protect themselves, but no one wants attention. And that gun they used made mincemeat of him, I hear. Who has a gun like that? It's about something else. Do you have a theory?"

"There's some superpatriots, white supremacists, who have guns like that," Schollmeyer said. "Did Steinmetz give offense to that crowd? Maybe on his show?"

The manager was pensive. "Short answer, yes," he said. "Longer answer, he gave offense to everyone. I couldn't keep his squabbles straight if you put a gun to my head. So to speak." He pointed his thumb over his shoulder at the bookcase. "I got seven years of Yosh tapes back there. You're welcome to give 'em a listen."

"I don't imagine you have transcripts?"

"Transcribed by whom?" the manager said. "We are proud to be public radio and poor as a church mouse."

Schollmeyer reflected ruefully that the Secret Service and Mendocino Public Radio shared resource constraints. His supervisors openly questioned whether he had his priorities right, and any attempt he made to secure additional support was quashed. Foster was in the same boat.

Schollmeyer had the name of the San Francisco guy who had found the body. He had checked him out—a solid citizen by all accounts. He called the guy's work phone and a Scandinavian-accented voice told him he had reached the New People's Garage. Schollmeyer asked for Spider Lacey, and the man said, "He's not here. Maybe I can help. What is the model and the problem?"

"It's not about a car. It's personal. When will Mr. Lacey return?"

"Monday."

"I would like to speak to him before then," Schollmeyer said. "Would that be possible, do you think?" He tried to sound neutral and friendly. A Minnesota boyhood had taught him something about Scandinavian intractability.

"No. He's not in town."

Schollmeyer felt his irritation rise. He could play the Secret Service card, but he didn't want to come on too strong. He wanted to see this friend of Steinmetz in person anyway, so he'd wait till Monday. "Maybe you could get him a message?" he said, as ingratiatingly as he could manage.

"What?"

Schollmeyer spelled his name and added his number.

Chapter 15

SOME OF THE SHINE HAD COME OFF REVEREND Footman for Cal. He talked a good game. He got people lathered up, and then boom, pound cake. Footman called *The Turner Diaries* "inspirational" but treated it like a fantasy. It was only a fantasy if they lacked the courage to make it real, Cal thought. Like he just had on the Calpella grade.

The big idea in Turner's book was that you had to make people choose sides: their own kind, or the rampaging horde of Jew-driven mud people. But the sheeple didn't see things as they were. Look what had happened in Clyde County, when the white bastion had come up for vote! The brainwashed fools had seen all the Pierces on the ballot and banded up to vote for the anti-Pierces.

They had two hundred and fifty voters where they used to have twenty. All the papers wrote it up as a victory for civil rights and American ideals—for the niggers and the Yids, in other words. To force people to choose, you needed to force the nigs to fight back, which would make the sheeple finally side with their own.

Cal thought about money all the time. The race war would call for some serious bacon; you couldn't fight the ZOG on a shoestring. But the reverend's mail-order sales produced nothing more than petty cash. And Kruger, the so-called counterfeiting ace, was a perfectionist washout. They were talking about starting with tens to lower the risk of passing the bills. You'd have to pass a hundred thousand ten-dollar bills to get a million dollars.

Cal had restrained himself for two weeks from making Reverend Footman or any other kinsmen directly aware of the haul from the Brink's job. It was common knowledge that the ZOG tapped the Ararat phone, along with Pastor Jack's and many others. Today, though, the reverend was going to preach at the Ukiah Church of Jesus Christ, Christian, and Cal was planning to share his news.

"Do you read the papers?" Footman barked. He held tightly to each side of the pulpit, as if only its ballast prevented him from being launched heavenward by the force of indignation. "Of course you do. Watch the TV? Of course, you do. So you know about our leaders apologizing that they are white, that they are in the image of God, apologizing even for their Christian faith. Can you believe that?"

He shook his head in amazement, and then shouted: "It is a sin to apologize for Christian Faith. It is Christian Faith which shall triumph, which shall administer justice all over the world in the time that is coming very soon! My brethren, we await the coming of the greatest right-winger of them all!"

Once, Cal had hung on every word. Now he tapped his foot.

Footman wound down, and then proceeded, beaming, down the aisle surrounded by congregants. Cal inserted himself and said in Footman's ear, "Reverend, we need to talk."

Footman smiled serenely and said to the others clustered around, "We got some coffee brewed up, and some of that pound cake that only Sister Eliza can make, may Yahweh smile on her. She said something about raisins in it this time. Go have yourselves some." The reverend led Cal into his office. "What's that?" he said, gesturing to the suitcase Cal was carrying.

"Three hundred and thirty thousand dollars, Reverend," Cal said. "A tithe."

Footman opened the suitcase and riffled through the top bills. "I can do a lot of good with this money."

"Reverend," Cal said, "seeing as it's just the two of us, where do you expect this money came from?"

"Either you manufactured it or you took it off the Brink's truck," Footman said.

"It's real."

"May I?" Footman said. He leaned over, extracted a bill, and held it up toward the light. He rubbed it and sniffed it.

"Don't just take my word for it," Cal said.

"Counterfeiting hundreds is risky. Every one will get checked."

"These are good," Cal said. "They don't keep records of these bills. They don't expect to be robbed."

Footman stared at the money. Finally, he said, "You were daring. 'Devote to destruction the sinners,' as Samuel said."

"So I have your blessing?" Cal said.

For several beats it was quiet, two men and a suitcase. Then the reverend said, "I am not sure we are ready for what you propose. For what you have already begun. If we move too soon, while we are not strong, we will be crushed."

"Behold," Cal said. "I send you out as sheep in the midst of wolves; so be shrewd as serpents."

Footman didn't relax his worried expression

"Look," Cal said. "We're not going to storm the mint. We know how to plan, and we know how to execute. We mean to set an example that others can follow. We need someone to tell the story. We need you."

"Can you be more precise about what you wish me to do?" Footman said.

"Five points to think about," Cal said. He held up his right hand and opened his thumb. "One, these are end times. We must prepare for high tidings and great deeds. You say that all the time already.

"Two, we are at war with Satan and we must smite or be smitten. Let us smite first.

"Three," Cal said, "He that hath no sword, let him sell his garment and buy one. That's Luke.

"Four, extol the patriots who raise the sword."

Cal paused, four fingers open and the little finger still closed. Footman looked at the hand and back at Cal. "You said there were five things to think about."

"Reverend," Cal said, "I can't save the race by myself. We need cells, like in the *Diaries*. We need patriots all over the country to pick up the sword."

"I would cut off my right arm if it brought Earl Turner's vision to fruition," Footman said, without enthusiasm. "And I commend you, son. I saw that you were special, which is why I anointed you to the Council. But what you are proposing, I don't know. The ZOG will respond in all its bestiality."

"I expect them to, once they figure out what's going on. But it will take them a while, and we shouldn't wait. Our tide is rising. Enough is enough, even for the sheeple. I have raised my hand, and it has not been cut off. Let many raise their hands. Some will fall, but more will rise."

Footman was silent. His gaze shifted from Cal to the open suitcase, to someplace in space above Cal's head. Finally, he said, "I would not hinder you, but what we have built here, at Ararat, we must preserve. We are a beacon that must shine through the long night."

"Of course," Cal said. "The last thing I want is to extinguish the beacon. You must stay above the battle. A wise man whom all look to."

That seemed to make Footman feel better. "What are you thinking specifically, Cal?" he said. "What do you want me to do?"

"Just run some ads, Reverend," he said. "Paid ads. And refer the right kinsmen in my direction."

The lawyer, Shelby, had submitted a bill for expenses that had floored the Reverend. "What do you have planned next?" Footman said. "If I may ask."

"You can ask," Cal said, "but it's better if I don't tell. We need to keep you representing the cause and out of jail. In fact, you might want to keep this tithing to yourself."

Footman could see the logic of that.

"I'll be sending you an ad," Cal said. "For your next edition."

•••

CAL WASN'T QUITE SURE HOW TO WORD THE ad. "Good men needed to rob armored cars and assassinate agents of the ZOG" was the gist of it, but you couldn't come right out and say that, even in Reverend Footman's newsletter.

He would have to word it carefully, so that those with eyes to see would understand, but the ZOG would not. His vision, like Earl Turner's, was of dozens, hundreds, thousands of cells bedeviling the ZOG until it knew not where to turn, and turned upon itself.

He felt good, driving home from the church. His wife had informed him that her potions had done the trick. His sense of obligation to his unborn progeny was boundless.

A kinsman who was employed at the Federal Reserve Bank in Missoula, Montana, had communicated that the bank held deposits for two weeks before conveying the funds to the larger federal bank in Des Moines. The Missoula kinsman had accumulated relevant sketches and timetables. A well-coordinated and armed group of twelve men could appropriate upward of eight million dollars on the second or fourth Thursday of the month. With eight million, Earl Turner's vision would be much less of a pipe dream.

His mood dampened when he thought about the responses he had received from his men about the new prospect. Thor and Odin had somehow both wedged into a payphone booth for the call; Cal couldn't get out of his mind the looks their combined five hundred pounds might attract.

"Earl," Thor had said, "before we get onto what comes next, we got some unfinished business about what we just pulled off. It ain't about the money, it's about how we make decisions."

"The way we make decisions just netted us three million," Cal said. "And a clean getaway."

"Ain't the point, Cal," Odin chimed in. "It's the principle of the thing."

"The principle of the thing," Cal said testily, "is that the ZOG is squeezing the life out of white people and I'm going to do something about it, whether you like my decision-making or not."

"Who anointed you Jesus Christ?" Thor said, and hung up.

Even Utah, usually acquiescent, was wary of the bank job in Missoula. They would have to coerce guards into giving up security codes. It could go terribly wrong. Still, Cal was bullish on their prospects. Missoula sat where three rivers and five mountain ranges converged. Kinsmen there would help them identify a secure place to camp while the police were swarming.

"Eight million dollars," Cal said to Utah. "I have a lead to a Syrian guy who sells KGB suitcase nukes for three and a half million. Can you imagine what we could do with a couple of those?"

With the right men, Cal felt sure, he could move mountains. He needed to find some better men who would appreciate his vision and help see it through.

Then there was the matter of Ernie Fresser going rogue and murdering the Jew. Ernie had taken to asking Cal at every opportunity if he'd seen The Man or, You Know Who, or once, on the phone, Mr. R., at which point Cal had lashed out at him for his indiscretion. Ernie was someone he could definitely do without.

He thought about Ricci, who should have contacted him by now with a thank you and a reward. Cal could appreciate the man wanting to lay low, but there had been time enough. If he didn't hear from Ricci this week, Cal decided, he would roust him out at the Fourth of July parade in Willits on Thursday.

Chapter 16

San Francisco, Monday, July 1, to Friday, July 5

AGENTS FOSTER AND SCHOLLMEYER KNEW FOR SURE THAT a series of seemingly unrelated events could be linked to a supremacist minister named Joseph Footman, who for the last two years had spent the bulk of his time in a fortified Nevada compound called Ararat. Schollmeyer carried a rolled-up wall chart from place to place, so he could add new tidbits from his investigation. Ararat was at the center of the chart, with arrows and cryptic runes connecting it to a host of other events, which were often connected with each other.

They had a source inside Ararat. The maintenance man there had broken a transvestite's face after encountering her penis. It was a gory case, an open-and-shut five-year sentence. The man was willing to wriggle out of it by keeping tabs for the feds on who was coming and going at Ararat. But he was on the periphery and never attended the meetings of the Council of Eight, where the decisions were made. Schollmeyer needed to turn the screws on someone closer to the core.

Finally, he'd caught a break. A Browning double-action semi-automatic had been found on the floor of the Brink's truck. The gun was registered in Laclede, Idaho. A warrant executed there yielded a pregnant wife, an asthmatic child, C-4 plastic explosives, dynamite, pipe bombs, hand grenades, fully automatic M-16 and AR-15 machine guns, sawed-off shotguns, pistols, crossbows, a Heckler and Koch Model 91 rifle in .308 caliber that had been illegally modified into a full automatic, ten .22 caliber Ruger target pistols fitted with integral silencers, three Ingram Mac-10 submachine guns with attached suppressors, and around a half ton of ammunition

It got better. Along with the weapons cache, they found plans to destroy both the Glen Canyon Dam switching yard and the Capitol Power Plant in Washington DC, complete with blueprints and diagrams of bomb placement. They found architectural renderings of DC's and New York's water supply, which connected, on Schollmeyer's chart, to two thirty-gallon cans of cyanide accidentally discovered two months before, while officers were serving a warrant for missed alimony payments in an Ozarks Posse Comitatus hideaway.

Foster was going to drum home to his superiors the scope of the destructive vision. Maybe he would make a dent this time.

They'd also found in Laclede a tiny notebook, which listed a series of code names along with a corresponding set of initials. It was a tantalizing breakthrough. Now, when they executed their wiretap on Reverend Footman, they could match Thor, Odin, Bayou, Bunyan, Utah, Hulk, Hoover, Kruger, Poundcake, Earl, and a half-dozen others to people with the right initials. Schollmeyer felt certain they could start holding some toes to the fire, if Foster could pry loose the resources.

These guys were following Earl Turner's playbook like it was a Betty Crocker recipe. They really thought they could cause a panic, bring down the government, and establish a white nation in the northwest. But Alex Schollmeyer wasn't going to let that happen.

He welcomed the Brink's holdup and even the Steinmetz murder as opportunities to track his quarry in the open field.

•••

WHEN SPIDER RETURNED HIS CALL ON MONDAY MORNING, Schollmeyer invited him to his borrowed office in San Francisco's Hall of Justice. Schollmeyer opened the door quickly to Spider's knock, shook his hand enthusiastically, motioned him to a chair and said, "Glad to meet you, sir."

"Glad to meet you too," Spider said. "Is this about Yosh? I didn't know the Secret Service got involved in local murders."

"Not normally, no," Schollmeyer said. "But we have reasons to believe that your friend's murder was committed by one or more of the people we are interested in from a much broader perspective." He looked at Spider intently, as if he expected him to know what he meant.

"Do you know what sedition means?" Schollmeyer asked.

"Sort of," Spider said. "Like treason, right?"

"Sedition means overthrowing our government," the agent said. "These guys are white supremacists. Aryans. Neo-Nazis. Klan. They're a serious threat."

"Why would they kill Yosh?"

"We're not sure. He was Jewish. Maybe he got in their face on his show."

"He got in everybody's face. What makes you think it was these people who killed him?"

"A fully automatic Ingram Mac-10 is not something you have lying around the house. It's a killing machine. These patriots stockpile 'em."

"So the sheriff has his head up his ass?"

Schollmeyer laughed. "To use the technical term, yes." He looked at Spider appraisingly. "I'm going to put some cards on the table, okay?"

"Okay."

"I'm reasonably sure you didn't kill your friend, and I need all the help I can get. So I am going to open my kimono, and I'm going to hope it sparks something on your end. Is that a deal?"

Spider briefly thought about the agent in a kimono. "Sure," he said.

"You read about this big armored car robbery?"

"Same crew?"

"Could be. There's one of these guys really catches the eye physically. He's got this big red Yosemite Sam beard down to his stomach. One of the lookouts on the highway had a beard like that. And when we showed the Brink's guard a picture of the Mac-10…" Schollmeyer produced a photo of something that looked more like a power tool than a gun. "The guy said, 'Bingo, they were waving that around.'" The agent said it all with great gusto.

"You knew him well," he said to Spider. "Any thoughts? Did he have any blowups with this crowd that you know about?"

"Among many others," Spider said. He told the agent about Yosh's files. "Your people could check them out, right?"

The agent's gusto receded. "Don't I wish," he said. "My FBI colleague and I are on the lonesome on this one. No infrastructure support."

They both pondered this, and then Spider said, "What about his listeners? He had a lot of them. I bet they'd want to help if they could."

The agent brightened. "I like it," he said. "Public is good. Make the perps nervous, make them show their hand. When can you do it?"

Spider had not expected to be issuing the appeal. The agent quickly added, "It's much more meaningful if it comes from his friend. Trust me."

"What am I asking people to do?"

"Remember shows where he really mixed it up with white racists. Call you with their leads. If something sounds serious, you call me, and I'll do my best to take a closer look."

"Why not call you directly?" Spider said. "That's your job, isn't it?"

"I only get so much time to work on this. Please try to understand."

Spider thought for a second and said, "Okay. I'll call the station manager. Can I say the Secret Service is on the case?"

"You bet!" Schollmeyer said. "I want to make these guys sweat, get them out in the light.

"Thank you," he added. "You might be saving our democracy."

Spider wondered what Yosh would think about that.

•••

SPIDER CALLED SIOBHAN AFTER HE PARTED WITH SCHOLLMEYER. She was enthused. She thought the Secret Service would operate at a higher level than the Mendocino sheriff's department. Spider called the station manager, who was happy to help. He said Spider could be on the morning show, the station's most popular, at 7:30 the next day.

It was still dark at 5:00 a.m. when Spider left San Francisco for Ukiah. There was no traffic, so he drank coffee in Ukiah for half an hour, rehearsing what he would say.

"A Mendolicious morning to all of you," the morning anchor opened. "We have a great show for you this morning. We'll be talking with the Willets-based author of the new book, *Men, They're Everywhere*, and we'll be following all the breaking news for you.

"First, though, let's take a moment to talk to Spider Lacey, a friend of Yosh Steinmetz who, as everyone knows, was brutally murdered near his home outside Ukiah just a little more than two weeks ago. According to the sheriff, there are no active leads in the case. Welcome, Spider."

"Thanks."

"You discovered Yosh's body?"

"Yes."

"I won't ask you what kind of shock that must have been. You've known Yosh a long time?"

"Since I moved to San Francisco, ten years ago. He helped me a lot."

"And you're on the show this morning why?"

"Well," Spider said. "We want to find out who killed him. Someone's walking around who did this thing."

"That's local law enforcement's job, right? The sheriff's office seems pretty convinced it was a pot murder."

"That's conceivable," Spider said. "It's not the only possibility."

"Yes?"

Spider had been squirming about how to play this moment. On the one hand, mentioning the Secret Service would get attention and Schollmeyer had told him to go ahead and do so. On the other hand, he had imagined himself a listener to the show, hearing some random guy blabbing about his Secret Service connection. It would have sounded bonkers. Since when did the Secret Service send mechanics on the radio to broadcast their investigations? Still, Schollmeyer was the pro.

"A Secret Service agent contacted me," Spider said. "They think this may have something to do with white supremacists."

"The Secret Service!" the anchor said. "That's heavy law enforcement machinery. And they sort of deputized you?"

"I know," Spider said. "It sounds weird. But it's true." He raised his eyebrows and spread his hands quizzically to signify to the anchor that he shared her incredulity. She was staring hard at him, trying to figure out if he were for real.

"Ok," she said. "The Secret Service and right wing crazies. I'll bite. And what do you, I mean what does the Secret Service, want our listeners to do?"

"They think it might have been someone he antagonized on his show."

"That would be half the county," the anchor said with a dry chuckle.

"Like I said, the agent particularly mentioned Aryans, white supremacists, people like that."

"Wow," the anchor said.

"The Secret Service wants to ask Yosh's listeners for help. I haven't listened to every show; we don't get the signal in the City. But lots of people up here have heard them all. Did anyone sound threatening on the air? Anything at all that might be a clue?"

"If people remember something, do they call the Secret Service?"

"Actually," Spider said. "They call me. I sort of collect the leads and sift them for the agent."

The anchor wrinkled her brow. She obviously was considering the possibility that Spider was delusional. "They're short-staffed on this," Spider said. "It's how the agent asked me to do it."

"Okay," she said. "Your tax dollars at work."

Spider gave his phone number, and the anchor repeated it. By the time he got home, he had twenty-four messages. People meandered all over the place. Their favorite memory was the one Yosh had loved, when he accused the anti-Semitic caller of masturbating for his race. A half-dozen callers harked back to the 1979 Greensboro Massacre, when the Klan killed Communist Workers Party protesters in North Carolina. Yosh had blamed the dead protestors for inciting brain-dead racists on their own turf. It was a "plague on both your houses" performance that had driven callers of all stripes apoplectic. But that was six years ago.

Two of the messages were from people who told him to watch out or he'd end up like his friend.

Spider decided to smoke a spliff, watch the news, and call it quits for the night. He couldn't find the remote, and then remembered it now lived under the TV, its cord neatly coiled around it. This was Siobhan's contribution to his décor; she had disentangled the spaghetti wires and run them under the rug. He couldn't deny it was an upgrade.

It could work financially for him to move to New York, Spider thought. He didn't relish the prospect, though. The thought of hiring on as a mechanic in somebody else's shop stuck in his craw; he had never worked for anyone else. He wished he and Siobhan had had more time to explore the natural wonderland outside San Francisco—climbing Mount Tamalpais, steelhead fishing on the Russian River, hiking Big Sur, kayaking in the Bay, bass fishing the sloughs of the Delta, camping in Yosemite and the Sierra Nevada. It would be hard for him to give that up.

She could be a lawyer here as easy as in New York, Spider thought—and, in the process, put a continent between her and that unpleasant Mel character. He felt helpless at a distance.

She'd said she'd try to come out Friday, but wasn't sure of her schedule. Sometime that weekend, in any case. He couldn't wait.

•••

Thursday night, the fourth of July, he could turn off his mind and play softball. He was allegedly the "automotive consultant" of a weekly alternative newspaper that thrived on investigative reporting and sex classifieds.

Spider was one of many ringers in the Media League, and Ohanian was another. Newspapers, radio stations, and cable TV outlets, big and small, private and public, left wing or merely liberal, competed and slept with each other, using the palette of co-ed softball.

Spider played short and batted cleanup for the Little Gorillas. Ohanian played center and led off. This night, for a change, they won.

Afterward, the team had the patio of the Connecticut Yankee to themselves. The night was warm for a San Francisco summer. The cocktails and beer were flowing, at the expense of the newspaper's publisher, who was over the moon about the victory. The men were beautiful, the women witty, and conversely. They had actually won! Ohanian was the hero; his diving catch saving the game. There were shots and toasts and group exultation.

Ohanian and Spider ended up seated at a table while the team cavorted around them, like fauns and nymphs around Apollo and Ares. One of the nymphs, the editor of the "Investigations" section, washed up to their table. "Great catch," she said to Ohanian. "You too," she said vaguely to Spider.

The publisher materialized, bringing celebratory shots to his star ringers. He was way past pain. "Aged agave," he said. "Fit for my gods." He toasted his gods and they toasted him back.

People were starting to peel away from the party. The Investigations editor resurfaced and said, "Is there anyone here who shouldn't be driving?" She looked at Ohanian.

"I shouldn't, I shouldn't!" Ohanian said.

They left immersed in warm colloquy. Spider trailed out behind them. Ohanian put an arm around the editor, turned her sideways, and pushed her left leg forward with his own. He guided her arms in the classic opposite-field hitting approach. There was unavoidable frottage; she was an avid student.

Behind his own car, Spider saw Ohanian's old BMW. The sidewalk sign said STREET CLEANING 8-10 FRIDAY. Ohanian would be out sixty-five bucks when he rolled out of the editor's bed in the morning.

The price we pay for love, Spider thought. He was glad to be getting off the singles treadmill at long last.

Friday morning, Agent Schollmeyer called him at the shop. "I forgot one thing," he said. "Be careful."

"Of what?"

"Well, you just told the Aryan world you think they're crazy. I'm not saying someone's coming after you in the middle of San Francisco but, you know, look both ways."

Here was the residue of Spider's time in Vietnam: he took danger seriously. Some people came back feeling indestructible, having made it through alive. Spider felt extremely destructible.

His life had been largely danger-free since Vietnam, but once, with Siobhan in Arizona, he had camped near an arroyo. Sometime after they had dozed off, he jerked awake, his brain frequency somehow permanently tuned to danger—in this case, the whistling sound of waters starting their mad descent. He had awakened Siobhan and packed their few things. They'd been on higher ground for only twenty minutes when the flash flood's waters cascaded over their previous camp. Spider was dismayed that he had let them camp there in the first place, but the weather had been fair, the stream had trickled prettily, and it had seemed pleasant to camp near it.

After the agent's call, Spider went upstairs to his flat and opened the bottom drawer of his dresser. He probed under the ironed shirts he never wore until he felt the outline of the combat medical badge he had been awarded, and then the handle of the hushpuppy, an Mk 22 nine-millimeter pistol with a tiny but effective silencer. Its distinctive, highly discreet belch was beloved by the army scouts, who used it to silence Viet Cong guard dogs and then their owners.

Spider hadn't looked at the badge or the gun for ten years. The badge featured a Greek cross, symbolizing the Geneva Convention, and entwined serpents, celebrating the badge recipient's cunning. Both motifs were superimposed upon a stretcher, which itself rested upon the Medical Corps insignia. An oak wreath, connoting strength and loyalty, completed the busy picture.

Spider put the badge back in the drawer and turned his attention to the beautiful little gun, just twenty-eight ounces and seven and a half inches long. Its silencer was a work of art, five inches long and just eight ounces.

Spider remembered winning it at the Camp Lejeune Hospital, bluffing with a high pair while the Navy SEAL four-flushed. When they showed their hands, the SEAL, loaded on painkillers, had put his head on the table and wept.

Spider re-examined the mechanism and then oiled it and put bullets in the eight chambers. He experimented with different ways of carrying the gun. Nothing worked until he remembered an old duster, which he finally found wedged in the closet. The gun fit easily in the capacious side pocket.

The hushpuppy fit his hand. In 1967, when he had looked at his low draft lottery number and then at his civil engineering reading list, he had decided to enlist as a medic, believing medics didn't carry weapons. Vietnam was the first war in which that wasn't so. He had come to appreciate guns.

Chapter 17

New York, Tuesday, July 2, to Thursday, July 4

IT SEEMED ODD TO SIOBHAN TO SEEK COUNSEL from someone ten years her junior, but Isabel possessed a huge supply of both savoir faire and sangfroid, qualities which Siobhan felt were sadly lacking in herself. She thought this was a function of Isabel growing up in the East Bronx and Siobhan in Kingman, Arizona. Isabel agreed that she was a much better judge of just about everything and did not hesitate to ladle out advice.

"Mel is not your problem," she told Siobhan.

They were eating gyros from a pushcart vendor near their office. The gyro filling oozed from the opening at the top like a melting ice cream cone. Siobhan licked away the yogurt and tabouli, trying hard not to drip.

Isabel took big bites, magically balancing the gyro so the ooze stayed in the pita. "Spider is your problem," Isabel said.

"You don't know what you're talking about," Siobhan said. "I like Spider. Could be love, even."

"Exactly," Isabel said. "And that's your problem."

When Siobhan looked blank, Isabel said in a voice suitable for a slow child, "You've got one more shot at the dream. Don't blow it for some sensory stimulation."

Siobhan had always assumed she would be a mother several times over, and a good one. Now, she was almost thirty-six and making money and could hardly fall asleep from the clamor of the ticking clock. Many women her age were in the same predicament. There was a certain bitterness toward men, or "worm boys" as they were derisively called, forever unable to commit.

"Spider," Isabel said. "Adorable in a kind of hunky, spectral way, but dad material? Think about it." Siobhan knew Isabel was upwardly mobile, and probably didn't think lawyers should mate with mechanics, but she might have a point. What had that ten years off been all about anyway? She had visited him as a lark, then came the murder, and now they were heading down the track like a runaway freight train. It occurred to Siobhan that she might be responding less to Spider and more to her own sense of desperation.

The truly odd thing was that when she thought about it, he seemed like perfect dad material—competent, steadfast, slow to anger, funny, at ease with himself. Plus, he woke up in a good mood most of the time. "He's got a lot of aplomb," Siobhan said. "That's a good dad trait, don't you think?"

"Aplomb!" Isabel said. She made it sound like a disease. "Look, girlfriend," she said. "You're done with Mel, you're clearing out some room, and you remember this nice hunky guy who was fun in bed. Why not? Some R and R. And then his friend gets drilled, and now you're co-starring in *Bonded by Tragedy*. I'm sorry, it's a bad movie. If the guy doesn't get killed, you're back home, ashes hauled, not giving old Spidey a second thought. Look, he gave you up for ten years; that ain't true love. Whew. I've said it."

"Yes, you have," Siobhan said.

"Besides," Isabel said, "One of you has to move and be miserable—what a great foundation for a marriage."

DANIEL BEN-HORIN

It was all extremely confusing and, in the meantime, there was Mel.

"He's playing nice now?" Isabel said, skeptical, after Siobhan told her about Mel's apology via her home screen. "Whatever. Like I said, he's not the problem. Just walk into that squat of his, sit him down, tell him you'll let him slide on the email hijacking but it's over, and that's that. And don't fuck him, please. Men are such simple creatures. They're prone to confusing sex with love."

Siobhan decided to confront Mel before the Elephant House dinner hour on Tuesday, but the managing director harried her and by the time she got to the squat, the evening festivities were in full flight. Mel rushed over to her, kissed her on the lips, and then returned to the simultaneous conversations in which he was engaged.

"What you need to do," he said to a young Latino guy, "is find a cross-subsidy building. You know what that is, right?"

The young guy didn't.

"It's a tax boondoggle," Mel said. "It lets developers do high-income construction and throw in some affordable apartments. A project like that's going to be in court for years. Great squat potential. The activists hate it." He drawled *activist* to show his disdain. The squatters thought the affordable housing nonprofits were way too cozy with the city.

A hulking young man appeared in the doorway and hoisted a toilet above his head in triumph. He was shirtless, and his pecs rippled with the exertion. Everyone clapped and cheered.

"All these new buildings have to install Gucci toilets and sinks. Low flow," Mel said to the Latino guy. "That's four great crappers we scored this week alone."

Nestor fluttered up to Siobhan. "Welcome back, lovely lady," he said. One of women of the squat, hugely pregnant, wearing a bra and carpenter's overalls gave her a big, sweaty hug. Siobhan thought things were going badly offtrack.

"Mel, let me ask you something," the young Latino guy said. "We got an army of homeless people outside our door…"

The man let the sentence trail off, but Siobhan understood the question. The squatter community was not the homeless community. Squatters had a home, and they often worked long hours making it livable.

"Listen," Mel said. "Let me tell you the number one thing to never, ever do if you want to survive. Don't let people in because you feel sorry for them. Just get all that liberal, idealistic bullshit out of your head. Squats attract deadbeats like bad meat attracts flies. You've got a core group of workers, and then you've got the parasites. It only takes a few parasites to turn everything to shit."

"These homeless people were rousted out of Tompkins Square," the woman who had hugged Siobhan said from across the table. "So we let them stay here. But they were addicts. You can't give people like that stuff for free, because they'll just crap on it. These guys were literally hanging their asses out the windows and shitting into the courtyard."

"You guys are way too nice," said a man Siobhan had never seen before. "I'd kick that hanging ass so hard, it wouldn't hang again, believe it." Everyone laughed, and in the banter that ensued, Siobhan gathered that the man was called Tramp.

It was time for dessert, a rich trove of pastries, the detritus of one of the French bakeries that were sidling eastward from Greenwich Village. A *Village Voice* reporter in a Euro-cut sport jacket hoisted a Napoleon on his fork and said, "How could anyone possibly call you guys yuppie parasites?"

"A toast," Mel said. He raised his glass, as did everyone else around the table. "To someone I love very much, who has returned after a brief hiatus. To Siobhan."

"To Siobhan!!"

Siobhan felt pissed, mainly at herself. She had wanted to end things quickly and quietly, but she'd allowed herself to be sucked into the vortex of an Elephant House dinner. Everyone was waiting, their glasses raised. She hoisted her own unsmilingly. Everyone cheered and drank.

Dinner took a long time. When the hubbub died down, she said to Mel, "Can we talk? Privately?" He led her to his office.

Once inside, she said, "Mel, I made a mistake…"

"I forgive you," he interrupted. "We all have spiders crawling around in our past."

"That's not what I mean," she snapped. "I didn't come here to make up. I made a mistake not being up front with you when things started to go bad between us."

"When was that?"

"I don't know, exactly, I didn't take notes. The point is, we're not right for each other."

"Except you like to fuck me? I feel used."

She laughed, knowing it was the wrong thing to do. "Oh, for god's sake, Mel, grow up. You used me for sex, and I used you. We used each other. It happened. It's over. Let go."

Mel didn't say anything right away. "Who's this Spider?"

"A guy I knew in Arizona. I broke it off to move here, but I guess I wasn't done with him."

"And you just, what, bumped into him on the street?"

"It doesn't matter how I ran into him. What matters is that I wasn't honest with you, and I'm trying to be honest now."

"So do you intend to keep using me?" Mel said. "I could be all right with some more usage…"

"No!" she said, more forcefully than she'd intended. "It would just muddy the waters."

"Sex with me is like muddy water?"

She could see he was not going to be reasoned into feeling okay. "Look," she said, "we had a nice time, and we can be friends if that works for you."

"If that works for me?" He looked bemused and a bit crazed. "No, I don't think so."

She couldn't think of anything more to say or do, so she said, "Bye, Mel," and left.

Nestor was waiting by the door to the office. He had a big smile for her, but she walked by him with her head down.

Nestor inched into Mel's office. "She not staying?"

Mel shook his head.

"Oh, no," Nestor said. "She got no right to do you like that."

They sat together silently, and then Nestor said, "Whatcha gonna do? Teach her a lesson? We could fuck that skank up bad."

Mel considered the notion and rejected it. "She deserves it," he said, "but I can't do it."

"What about him?" Nestor said. "Teach him not to fish in your pond."

As soon as Nestor spoke, the idea came fully formed into Mel's brain. It wouldn't bring her back, but it would feel awfully good.

•••

SIOBHAN CALLED ISABEL AS SOON AS SHE GOT home from Elephant House. She was upset, but it was all in a day's work, for Isabel. "Good cojones, girl," she said. "One down, one to go."

Still, Siobhan felt lousy. She had hurt someone who had given her quite a bit of pleasure and done her no harm until provoked. She had been careless, and she reproached herself for it.

There was a jokey message from Spider on her machine, wondering if she'd made a flight reservation. Siobhan thought about what Isabel had said. Isabel was annoying in her self-confidence, and her own love life was a rinse and repeat of fiery breakups and dramatic reconciliations with a rotating squad of lovers, but still.

New York was Siobhan's home now. She wasn't going to flee Mel for Spider's San Francisco arms. She drank a glass of wine and couldn't quite bring herself to return Spider's call before she fell asleep.

At work the next morning, Isabel walked over to her desk and said, "Make a friend for life?"

"We already are," Siobhan said.

"Not me. Iris. Her kid got kicked out of Horace Mann, and she's got a real bad case of single mom blues."

Iris was a more senior lawyer in the firm. "What does that have to do with me?" Siobhan asked.

"Iris has these interviews set up on the chemicals case, in Arizona and New Mexico, but she needs to stay here and beat the crap out of Junior."

"Sure, I'll do it," Siobhan said. "When are we talking about?"

"That's the thing," Isabel said. "She's got it set up for Saturday afternoon. As in three days from now. Something to do with college football. She says it was hard as hell to get it set up and she needs someone to be there."

"I'll go," Siobhan said.

"I would," Isabel said. "Get shut of those boys, do some work, clear your head. You got a very unclear head right now, girl, if you don't mind my saying so."

"You are so right," said Siobhan. A new idea had come to her. Take a break. Drive through the Southwest. Clear her mind in the desert.

Spider would understand. If he didn't, that would tell her something too. The more Siobhan thought about it, the more it seemed to her that her life had been defined by men, in the sense that they were always there, like refrigerators. She tuned her fantasy to "solo road trip" and it felt good. It was time for a timeout from men. Time to reflect, reset. If she were going to throw in with Spider, she wanted it to be for the right reasons.

•••

TRAMP THE ADDER SWUNG BY ELEPHANT HOUSE OFTEN, throwing his considerable self into whatever building project was going on and getting along with everyone.

On the Fourth of July, the residents partied on the roof. Tramp brought a bunch of other Adders to check out the scene, along with a keg and coke for all. Tramp put a big mellow arm around Mel's shoulders and told him he was the man.

Mel accepted the compliment modestly. He had something he wanted to discuss with the biker, but Tramp beat him to it.

"Your girlfriend is one fine piece," Tramp said. "You're a lucky dog."

"She is fine," Mel said. "And I was lucky. Then I got busy and some yuppie dickwad snuck in behind my back."

"You're not going to sit still for that, man!" Tramp said.

"I'm trying to figure out how best not to sit still," Mel said. "You got any ideas?"

As Mel expected, the topic was catnip to Tramp. "We got a thing called Adder Revenge," he said. "When some skank gets out of line, a bunch of boys pay her a visit."

"Actually," Mel said, "my beef is with the guy."

"No problem. How big is your beef?" Seeing Mel's confusion, he simplified: "You want him dead?"

Mel hadn't considered that. He had a better chance of Siobhan returning if the competition were eliminated. On the other hand, murder tended to elicit the best efforts of law enforcement.

When he thought about it, he didn't really want her back. She wasn't the person he had believed her to be. "No," Mel said. "Not quite dead."

"Got it," Tramp said happily. "Leave it to me."

Chapter 18

THE HANDYMAN AND ASSISTANT THAT ESTEBAN HAD PROMISED Julie turned out to be Esteban. He showed up in a pickup wearing work clothes. The bed of his pickup was piled with rakes, a weed whacker and other tools.

"Super verisimilitude," Julie said.

She expected an uncomprehending smile, but Esteban said, "Yes, verisimilitude, exactly. People see what they expect. Just like you did the other day." His affect was serious, totally different from the low-wattage guy he had played two nights before.

"Huh!" Julie said. She stared at him and he stared back. "So who the fuck are you? No offense."

"None taken," Esteban said. He had brought bags of groceries, which he stowed in the refrigerator and the cupboard. Julie saw some Fauchon mustard and what looked like smoked salmon. "You are familiar with the FMLN, I assume," he said.

Julie was, sort of, in an acronym-challenged kind of way. It pretty much buggered the brain to keep the FMLN, the FSLN, and the FALN straight. The FMLN was the one that bombed bars in New York to support Puerto Rican independence, she was pretty sure.

"Of course," she said.

"And Pablo Escobar, the name means something to you?"

Julie knew about the Medellín Cartel and its mixed reputation. Policemen, judges, journalists killed, yes, but also schools and football fields built and people fed. Sort of like Colombian Panthers, but with more drugs and money. Julie's illness had accelerated her radicalism; her time was likely not going to be very long, and she wanted to see as much as possible changed while she was still around to witness it.

"I can't wait to see where you're going with this," Julie said.

Esteban laughed. He seemed very relaxed and quite charming. "El Patron, Pablo, funds the rebels. I am his emissary. Naturally, this is not widely known."

"You do this emissary work in California?"

Esteban laughed again. He had remarkably white teeth. "For the moment, I am on a special assignment. El Patron loves the finest things. Yosh's pot is a finest thing. Now that Yosh is dead, I have to ensure continuity of supply."

"So he wants to resurrect Yosh's business?" Julie said. "Coals to Newcastle, if you know the expression."

"I studied two years at the London School of Economics, so I'm comfortable with Anglicisms," Esteban said. "Marijuana is more subtle than coal. Yosh's is very subtle. We do not know how to do this in Colombia yet."

"So you go to all this trouble..." Julie made an encompassing notion with her hand.

"In Medellín," Esteban said, "we trade a whole ounce of cocaine straight up for an ounce of what Yosh grew. Supply and demand. It is a special thing, this weed. Totemic, you might say. Girls want it before they..." He suddenly grew shy, which Julie thought was kind of cute. "Obviously, it is not the climate," Esteban said. "A light bulb is a light bulb. But there is some secret Yosh had. Fertilizer, maybe. Or technique. Light and dark, the ratio. We need to know this."

"You think he left a manual?"

"Why not? It was a lot to remember. But even if not, he had equipment, he had a helper. We will figure it out."

"You went to LSE," Julie said. "Did you know Mick Jagger?"

"I am not that old," Esteban said. "I am more like your age."

Julie knew Mick's age because they shared a birthday, although he was a year younger. She figured Esteban to be about ten years younger than herself, in his early thirties perhaps. She recognized that Esteban was beginning to flirt. She found the concept intriguing.

•••

A PLEASANT SURPRISE! ESTEBAN PROVED WONDERFUL IN BED, not at all like the lousy Latin lover stereotype. In the morning, he brought coffee to her in bed, and she said, "Do you know what today is?"

"Thursday!" he said. "What do I win?"

He reached out to her in the bed, but she rolled away and said, "Señor! I am deathly ill! Have mercy."

"You were fine last night," he said. "All night."

It was true. She had been very fine last night, but it was also true that she wasn't feeling sexual this morning. It was the nature of the disease.

"You've weakened me with your onslaughts," she said, trying to keep things light. "And today is not just Thursday. It is Independence Day, when we celebrate our freedom to enslave and torment others. It's a big national party."

"I know this holiday," Esteban said. "It is the one with the bad sausages in the soggy buns."

"That's pretty much all of them, but yes," Julie said. "And flags and firecrackers and beer. And parades! I bet there's a parade we can go to. Let's!"

Esteban loved the County Fair. He couldn't get enough of the rigged carny games: the Milk Bottle Pyramid, with its lead-bottomed bottles; the Basketball Shoot, with its oval rim and superinflated ball; and Shoot the Star, with the tampered rifle sights.

In her chair, Julie convulsed with laughter. "*Caro*," she said. "*Estúpido*. They're all fixed. You're throwing away money." He eventually amassed enough points to win a large stuffed pink moose, vaguely modeled on Bullwinkle, which she held in her lap as he wheeled her through the 4H exhibits.

When they got back to the house, he picked her up and carried her into the bedroom. She was aroused, but weak. "Don't do anything, *mi encantadora*," he said. "Just lie back and be beautiful." He lavished her with attention and then she brought him to orgasm with her hand.

Esteban had soft matted black hair that covered his chest, stomach, and legs. When Julie threaded her fingers through his pelt, he said, "Some women only like smooth men."

Julie thought that was adorable. "Well, you better stay away from those women," she said. "I'll keep you hidden here, so they don't hurt your feelings."

He laughed more than the remark merited. "You are wise, Julie, more than you know." He was pensive, and then said. "I will tell you my little true story now, yes?"

His little true story, for starters, had nothing to do with Pablo Escobar, who operated in the north of Colombia, in Antioquia and Santander states, far from Esteban's home, Cali, in the Southwest.

Nor did it concern the FMLN, which turned out to be Salvadoran, not Puerto Rican.

Esteban had, in fact, attended L.S.E., thanks to the munificence of his older brother, whom Esteban referred to by his cartel name, El Científico. His brother had smitten his enemies and amassed wealth, but his reign was unexpectedly cut short by his overconfidence, resulting in a US arrest. The feds had convinced El Científico to sing lustily in exchange for a reduced sentence. His information led to dozens of arrests.

The relatives and business colleagues of those arrested had reacted poorly to El Científico's defection. Esteban told Julie about his four cousins, tortured and executed by the "Elite Antiratas." He smiled incongruously and said, "I was next."

"I'm so very glad you're alive," Julie said. She moved toward him on the bed and took his temporarily flaccid penis in her mouth. He gripped the side of the bed with both hands and his whole body went rigid while she made him come. She swallowed his semen and said, "Maybe it will be a miracle cure."

They cuddled peaceably, and then Esteban said, "I haven't been so glad to be alive. It is hard to be a vanished man."

He told Julie that the massacre of his cousins had caused him to flee to the States. No one knew his whereabouts. "So it cannot be tortured from them."

Yosh's pot had been his source of income and his ticket off the death list. "We don't have Sinsemilla in Colombia. That part was true," he said. "It is very rare. The people who wish to kill me are connoisseurs. I have sent them gifts and asked if I can atone for my brother."

"What did they say?" Julie asked.

"They said there is much to atone for. They want the pot. I need to keep them happy until El Científico gets out of jail, three more years."

"What happens then?"

Esteban looked at her like she was simple. "We kill them, of course. It is what I dream about." She startled, and he added, "What I dreamt about, I mean. Now I dream about you."

•••

IN THE MORNING, SHE DROVE DOWN TO THE city to see her doctor. Her specially configured van had decimated her trust fund ten years ago. Now the van was getting creaky, and Julie wasn't feeling so well herself.

New MS symptoms had started to crop up unpredictably. Some days her left side was numb; other days her vision was blurred, or her fingers tingled constantly, or moving her neck felt like getting an electroshock. She was tiring more easily, and when she wasn't tired, she was dizzy. Her bowel and bladder had agendas of their own. She'd had tests done a week before, and this visit was to go over the results.

The doctor was willowy and blonde, a little like Julie, only healthy and optimistic. She had a picture of a wholesome husband and two kids on the wall between her degrees.

The results weren't good—Julie had either primary regressive or secondary regressive MS. She could hope it was secondary and that the symptoms would remit. But even if they did, the doctor said, they would return, and more virulently.

If it were primary regressive MS, she was commencing an irreversible downward slide.

"I know how hard this is to hear," the doctor said, her face exuding sympathy.

"You don't know shit," Julie said, and spun her wheelchair around and out the door. She had been planning to visit with San Francisco friends, but she wasn't in the mood anymore. She got in her van and drove back to Ukiah, glad that Esteban would be there.

Chapter 19

THE BATHROOMS AT FARNESE MIO WERE ROCOCO AFFAIRS. Bill Ricci watched in the gilded mirror as blood spurted out of his neck. He wiped off the shaving soap with a towel, dabbed the cut dry, and daubed it with a styptic pencil until a crust formed and the bleeding stopped. Ricci loved to shave and had invested in a shaving brush with jaguar bristles. Shaving was an opportunity to admire his healthy reflection and contemplate his day. But today's contemplation was sullied. He was in all the papers, and not in a good way.

It was John McEnroe's fault. The tennis bad boy had torn off his shirt and cursed a referee. As a member of the governing board of the United States Davis Cup, Ricci was a loud proponent of traditional tennis decorum. His media guy had arranged a conference call for him to condemn McEnroe, but the reporter from the *Chronicle* had blindsided him, asking if it weren't hypocritical to castigate the tennis player while being on the receiving end of a sexual discrimination suit from his longtime executive assistant. The reporter had invited him to expound on his "moral calculus." Ricci had tried to brush off the question with a joke about not getting that far in math, but the damage was done.

They'd been negotiating privately with Heather's attorney, trying to figure out how much it would take to make her go away, but word had obviously leaked out.

Ricci liked to brag about Heather's memory and efficiency. And she wasn't a dog either, though a little undersized in the mammilla department, as Ricci had informed the audience at his stag dinners. He joked that he thought it hurt Heather's feelings that he didn't hit on her, the way she cocked her snoot at him when he was flirting with the admins who passed through the Redwood Pacific executive suite on brief tenures.

Ricci treated the girls first-class, he told his dinner guests. He gave them generous checks and many of them wanted another helping. Heather cut all the checks.

Her feelings had indeed been hurt, it turned out, but not in the way Ricci had imagined. Her suit detailed a Rabelaisian workplace. Ricci was right about her memory.

The cut started oozing again. Ricci flicked at the caked alum, then reapplied the styptic. He decided to wear a light linen suit to the Fourth of July parade in Willits. He knotted a knit burgundy tie, brushed his silver hair, and gave ten strokes to each side of his Gable-inspired mustache. It would be odd to appear in public without Heather hovering somewhere nearby.

Ricci's team was to meet him in the Willits main square at eleven. The plan was to sample the Fourth of July joys of the County Fair and then proceed back to Farnese Mio to relax by the pool. Waiting for his people to assemble, Ricci perused the morning gymkhana— horses and riders competing at the 5-Can Barrels, Washington Poles, and Turn and Burn courses. He smiled left and right, but no one made eye contact, let alone came up and shook his hand, as people usually did.

It was about the Steinmetz murder. People thought he was behind it. It still amazed Ricci that Cal Albright had followed through, so quickly and decisively. Now there was the matter of the reward. It couldn't be soon and it couldn't be traceable. Nothing connected Ricci to the killing except Cal's say-so, and Ricci was determined to keep it that way.

His team showed up and wished him the best. A team social occasion was something to be looked forward to, or else. When Ricci saw Cal Albright, he took him by the arm and drew him into Neeta's coffee shop. After they had established that the weather was good and after Neeta had slammed two cups of coffee in front of them, Cal said, "Took care of that little thing for you, Mr. R.?"

"Before you go on," Ricci said, "I've got something to tell you. Your work as a labor contractor is outstanding, and the company and I value you more than we can possibly put into words." He stared into Cal's eyes. "I wouldn't even *try* to put it into words, if you follow me."

Cal didn't blink. "Well, that's great," he said. "It's great to be appreciated. It's great to be appreciated tangibly."

"Isn't it!" Ricci agreed, as if Cal had come up with an important new idea. "And you will be, you have my word on that. Have I ever steered you wrong?" he added. Cal still looked dour.

"Mr. Ricci, they're waiting…" This from his acting admin, who had inserted her upper frame inside the coffee shop door. She was very good-looking.

"I'm on the reviewing stand," Ricci said to Cal. "Whoopee." He clapped Cal on the back and made his way rapidly out.

Neeta brought the check in his wake. "Big spender," Neeta said.

•••

CAL PAID THE BILL, MOROSE. HE HAD THREE million dollars at his disposal, but he didn't like getting stiffed. He could hear the parade's trombones ooom-pah-pahing further up Main. He left the coffee shop and wandered toward the noise. He could see the marchers now, the pompoms flying in the air, the snare drum and trombones and Sousaphone tuba making a racket.

"Lookit there," said a familiar voice to his right. It was Ernie Fresser, directing Cal's attention to a high-stepping, very young majorette. The girl was all in red—fez, cape, jacket, short skirt, socks, shoes—except for a white cane and white flounced bloomers, which punctuated every marching step. Cal thought she was awful young to be flouncing her bloomers like that.

"My little girl," Ernie said. "Won a talent contest, can you believe it?"

As soon as the majorette's contingent had passed, Ernie said to Cal, "Keep expecting to hear from you."

"Yeah," Cal said. "I keep expecting to hear too. I just had a little chat with him. He's good for it."

"I thought it was c.o.d.," Ernie said.

"Who said that?" Cal replied. "I told you not to get any ideas. Just keep your trap shut while I work this out."

Ernie's mouth opened and then closed without any sound issuing forth. He looked like a large-mouthed bass. It was a shame, Cal thought, for the new Earl Turner to be surrounded by dull tools.

A loud, enthusiastic voice said, "Cal Albright, how ya doin'?" and then, "Ernie," with much less excitement.

"Hopalong," Cal said. "I'm surviving. How's yourself?"

Ernie slunk off with a hangdog look. Sheriff Cassidy beamed at Cal, whose connection to Ricci and the gyppo clans made him someone worth getting along with. "Well," he said, "other than being toasted over an open flame by the Secret Service over this Steinmetz case, I'm bearing up."

"Secret Service?" Cal said. "What would they care about a pot murder? Don't they have the president to protect?"

Hopalong tapped the side of his nose twice with his forefinger. "Don't let it get about, Cal, but they think it's not about pot. Maybe a political thing." He looked around to reinforce the confidential nature of his disclosure. "Aryans," he said portentously. Then he laughed. "Whatever the hell that means. My view is, Steinmetz gave someone short weight or bum weed, and they didn't want it to happen twice. Sometimes you don't have to make things complicated, know what I'm saying?"

Cal said he knew exactly what the sheriff was saying. His contempt for Ernie Fresser was increasing by the minute. Here they were, fighting for the race, and he was liable to take them all down over a grudge. Earl Turner didn't have to deal with stuff like that.

Chapter 20

New York and Kingman, Arizona, Friday, July 5, to Saturday, July 6

SIOBHAN PREPPED FURIOUSLY FOR HER MEETINGS. AT THE core of the case was DBCP, a chemical that was being linked with workers' sterility at nonunionized plants in the Southwest. These plants dealt with thousands of chemicals that were regulated by OSHA, which established the level of worker exposure that was safe in each case. Standards had been assigned to five hundred chemicals, a fraction of those in use. DBCP, which was used to control root-attacking nematode worms, had not been assigned a standard.

Iris had recorded and transcribed her exchange with an OSHA official:

"The ones that have standards are the ones that have problems, and that's why they have standards," the OSHA man said.

"DBCP—there's no standard, and there's a problem, it seems," Iris said.

"And now there will be a standard," the OSHA official said. "Because we got a problem."

It was a great case. There was a chain of complicity extending from the various operators of the mixing plants right up to Dow Chemical. The plants were outside small desert towns of conservative people who welcomed any addition to their tax base. The only worrisome part of the case was that the workers themselves were macho archetypes. The meetings Iris had arranged were meant to enthuse them about the case, so they would stand together as a class.

In Iris's notes, Siobhan found a transcription of a conversation with the general manager of the plant in Bisbee.

"What was your initial feeling when you first found out that in fact these men were sterile?" Iris had asked.

"Shock," the man said. "We had no idea. We had no idea at all that we had any kind of process here in our plant operations that could do such a thing to a human being."

"But what about the study done by Dow back in 1961 that indicated DBCP caused sterility in rats?"

"The Torkelson study!" the plant manager said. "Yes, we knew about that. But it did not show sterility in rats. What it showed was that with very high doses of DBCP you could get testicular atrophy. I've talked with two scientists and they both say, 'Heck, we just didn't draw the conclusion that there'll be sterility from the fact that the testicles were shriveling up.'" Iris had typed HECK AND DOUBLEHECK after the entry. It was definitely a winnable case.

The call to tell Spider that she wouldn't be coming out kept being the next thing she would do. Then it was Friday and she was running for the airport early in the morning, and then she really had to put pedal to the metal to get to Kingman, three hours north, for dinner with her dad at five thirty, which was what he considered dinnertime.

Dinner with Dad had been a late addition to her agenda. She hadn't seen her father in twelve years, even before she moved to New York. But she had been thinking about him, off and on, for a month, since reconnecting with Spider. It had struck her that the two had much in common; they were both auto mechanics, big reliable men. As a girl, she could count on her dad being a rock. She had similar feelings about Spider, with the annoying geographical caveat. So was she trying to mate with her dad? That was bad, right?

•••

On March 17, 1956, two days before Siobhan Mollenkopf's sixth birthday, her mom, Sinead Gleason Mollenkopf, had volunteered to run down to the wholesale auto supply place on East Andy Devine Boulevard to get some valve covers. She was going to combine the trip with some grocery shopping.

On the way, Sinead saw a large crowd gathered and stopped to see what was going on. Never shy, she had edged her way to the front to get a good view of a propane fire that was raging around a railroad car.

"Damn fool sparked it," a man next to her said, explaining that a railroad worker had attempted to tighten a leaking transfer valve connection by hitting a wrench with another wrench.

The Kingman Fire Department had responded, and firefighters were setting up attack lines to cool the propane car. As the crowd watched, the safety valve opened from the increased pressure inside the tank car. A stream of propane gas blew out and ignited as well.

It was quite a sight, a fiery cross—one stream of blazing propane shooting vertically out of the car from the safety valve, another burning stream discharging horizontally from the transfer valve. The brilliant cross drew cries of "Praise Jesus" and "Hallelujah."

The fire department decided to set up a deluge gun to cool the car, but before they could, the tank car exploded. Thousands of gallons of boiling liquid propane gasified and ignited. The remains of the rail car were propelled over a quarter mile.

One of the shards hit Sinead Mollenkopf and killed her instantly. Nine other people were killed and more than a hundred were injured. Film of the event became essential in the "what not to do" sections of firefighting training materials.

The coincidence of his wife's death and his only child's birthday almost crushed Jim Mollenkopf. But he had borne the weight, and Siobhan remembered him as the best dad ever during her childhood years. He never remarried, although any number of Kingman women considered him a catch, with his prosperous auto repair establishment strategically located on historic Route 66, not far from where Kingman ends and the desert begins, next stop LA, three hundred miles due west. "You *might* make it without a valve job, could happen," her dad would murmur to travelers who made the mistake of asking the big reassuring man in the wire rim glasses to take a quick look under the hood. Jim would brag of the expensive, gratuitous repairs he had foisted on those travelers, but he made a point of never fleecing the locals, and people respected him for that.

Jim did everything he could for Siobhan, and Siobhan quickly figured out that the way she could repay him was to be as much as possible like a boy. Jim loved to fish and hunt, and was happy when Siobhan said she wanted to come too. He was dazzled at how quickly she picked things up. She could bounce a Humpy Adams Hairwing in a sun-dashed stream so that a trout had no choice but to gobble it up. She didn't take to shooting animals, but at target shooting she was a natural. Jim hung her targets with their riddled bullseyes around his shop, a great conversation-starter with his marks.

The closest thing they had to a fuss happened during a fishing trip in her junior year in high school. Jim, with a few beers in him, started unloading on some saguaros. Siobhan's natural sciences teacher had shown the students a film called *Desert Under Threat,* which had been particularly scathing about saguaro assault, a viewpoint she conveyed to her father.

Her dad had exploded. A lot of stuff she'd never heard before came tumbling out. He didn't trust public school teachers who worked for the government, which was controlled by the Jews who took all the money, which was why the fire trucks in 1956 didn't have the right equipment to stop the catastrophe that had taken her mom. He was shaking with rage by the time he was finished. He took a walk by himself. When he returned, he was normal.

She still felt contentious. "Dad," she said, "I'm going to be a scientist when I grow up and save the saguaros."

He laughed and said, "Honey, you can be whatever you want. Hell, you can be president," and gave her the biggest old hug.

She stayed as close to home as possible for college, going to Arizona State even though she had the grades for out-of-state, even Ivy League. In March of 1968 came the news of the My Lai massacre, and the campus erupted. She was swept up in something much bigger than herself. When spring break came, she didn't feel like partying. She felt obliged to go home and share her convictions with her father.

It was a short visit with a long consequence. He responded that war was war, Communists were the enemy, and Lieutenant Calley deserved a medal of honor. For good measure, he added he had a mind to yank her out of that Commie-infested college he called A.S. Jew and put her to work in the front of his shop, where he could keep an eye on her.

Siobhan gathered her things and drove the three hours back to Tempe. She took out a loan and found part-time waitressing work. Upon graduation, she became a probation officer for the City of

Phoenix. When Siobhan decided to move to New York, she let her dad know via her annual Hallmark Christmas card, four months after the fact.

Driving to Kingman now, she thought about the rift with her dad that had opened after My Lai. Neither would bend. They had divorced. But even a divorced couple can become friends again. In New York, she had met people who'd broken with their parents and then found some common ground again much later. He wouldn't be around forever, and he'd been a wonderful father when she needed one.

She had called her dad on Thursday, telling him that an emergency case had come up in Arizona and she could drive down and have dinner with him on Friday, sorry for the short notice. She had a meeting the next day in Bisbee, so it would be a quick visit.

Her father just said, "That'll be fine, honey. Where do you want to eat?" as if she'd been keeping up with Kingman cuisine while in New York.

"Is the Cattleman still there?" she asked. She had dined there once or twice a week after her mom died. The waitresses collectively adopted her, and a couple of them would have adopted her dad too, if he'd shown any interest.

"It surely is," he answered. She could hear the pleasure in his voice. "Didn't expect you still ate meat."

"I'll eat a steak with *you*," she said. He barked a laugh of appreciation. He'd been forty-two when she was born, so he was pushing eighty now. He sounded strong on the phone.

The plan was to have dinner with her father, sleep in a motel, and then set out for the six-hour drive to Bisbee, near the southern border of the state. Then she would drive another five hours to Alamogordo, New Mexico, to meet with a different set of workers. And then....it wasn't entirely clear to her. She'd heard that the

Colorado high country near Durango was exceptionally pretty. She'd brought her fly rod, which had sat in its case for ten years. She'd rent a little cabin, she thought, listen to the Kate Wolf song about the Great Divide, get her head on straight. She loved that song.

•••

SHE GOT TO KINGMAN WITH A LITTLE TIME to spare and called Spider from the Amoco station. She knew he wanted to be with her and she felt the same, but she had made her decision and she was going to stick to it. She knew it was going to be hard to explain.

Spider was so cheerful to hear from her, and then, when he realized what she saying, he got hurt and quiet. "You've got to trust me, Spider," she said. "This is about me, not about you."

There was some dead air, and then he said, "Okay, have a good trip."

She hung up. She'd meant to ask him about the response to his radio appeal, but she didn't feel like calling back.

Her father was sitting in a rust-colored leatherette booth when she arrived and rose to meet her. She'd conditioned herself to expect physical diminishment. Instead, he loomed larger than ever. Only the slack skin on his face betrayed his age. He seemed unsure about how to greet her but melted inside her hug. "My little girl," he said. "Emma! Chloe! Marianne!"

She had dined at the Cattleman on the night of her high school graduation. She'd ordered her usual Shirley Temple, but the waitress brought her a dirty Shirley instead, with vodka, colluding with her dad. She'd spit out her first sip, everyone laughing and having a ball.

The old waitresses were still there, the three women who'd made her feel special. Chloe, always the sauciest, made her stand up and turn around to be inspected. "Bet your clothes cost more than I made last month," she finally said. "You look good, lady."

Siobhan and her dad made small talk about the town. It was amazing how little had changed. There was a Walmart now.

Siobhan reckoned there was no point in delaying her prepared remarks. "Dad," she said, "there's something I've been meaning to say to you." She could see the veins on his temples enlarge. He clearly thought it was going to be bad news, like marrying a Jew or a black man. "Thank you," she said. "That's all."

She picked at the croutons in her salad. When he didn't say anything, she continued, "Thank you for being the kind of dad you were to me after Mom died. I was the best taken care of little girl in Kingman, and I don't believe I ever thanked you."

Tears were flowing unstanched down his cheeks. Hers too. Emma, Chloe, and Marianne stood together at the cash register unabashedly observing, puddling up themselves. "Honey," her dad finally said. They held hands across the table. Their rib eyes and baked potatoes arrived and they ate in silence, neither wanting to break the moment.

After he'd given Chloe their dessert order, he said, "You're not going to stay in that motel, are you? I ain't changed a thing in your room."

It had been Siobhan's firm resolve to not spend the night under her dad's roof. "I'd love to," she said.

The house, in the nice section of town shielded by a big butte from the worst of the high desert sandstorms, looked pristine: the grass watered and mowed, the oleanders trimmed. Her dad had told her on the ride over that he'd sold the business and had "enough to get by and a little more."

She asked him how he spent his time, and he said, "I'll show you."

Inside, the house looked the same, with the notable exception of the IBM XT that sat on the dining room table. "Wow, Dad,

I'm impressed," Siobhan said. "You're a modern man. More than my boyfriend."

Jim sat down in front of the computer. There was a pen and pad and magnifying glass neatly lined up next to the computer. "Here's how I spend my time," he said.

Siobhan heard his modem buzzing and connecting.

"You got a fella, eh?" he said. "What's he like? Where'd you meet him?

Siobhan had not expected to be discussing Spider with her father. "We met ten years ago, actually, in Arizona," she said. "Then I went to New York and he went to San Francisco. Just recently we sort of reconnected."

"Huh," her dad said. "That ten years off stuff makes me think you had your doubts."

"It's complicated," she said. "You didn't marry Mom till you were forty."

"I didn't give her ten years off once I met her, I can tell you that."

"Well, I like him now," Siobhan said. "A lot. You'll never guess what he does for a living." Her father didn't show any signs of guessing. "He runs an auto repair shop, just like my dad," Siobhan said. "What do you make of that?"

"Huh," her father said. "Would of thought you could aim higher. Fella got a name?"

"His name's Jeremiah," Siobhan said.

"Jeremiah," her father said. "The prophet of doom. Not very cheerful."

"Well," Siobhan said, "nobody calls him that. His nickname's Spider."

"Spider," her father said. He muttered to himself and pecked at his keyboard. He found what he wanted and scrolled down, reading.

"He specializes in Citroëns," Siobhan said, and then remembered that her father loathed foreign cars and the people who drove them. And long hair. She didn't think her dad would like Spider very much.

"Do you still think about Mom?" Siobhan said.

The question seemed to surprise him. "Still think about her?" he said. "I've thought about her every day for twenty-nine years. Hell, I got to think of her, because she's my password."

"I don't even have any photos," Siobhan said. "I remember she had a lot to say. And a big laugh."

"A lot to say!" her dad said. The thought amused him. "That woman could talk the paint off a wall. And she was funny. She made me laugh; she had that Irish whatchamacallit, the same thing you have. When you walked into that restaurant, I thought I was seeing a ghost."

He thought for a few seconds, and then said, "Come on back to the bedroom, I got something to show you." In the bedroom, he went to the closet and took out a small steamer trunk. Inside were photo albums, each neatly labeled with dates. "Help yourself," he said. He picked up one of the books and quickly became lost inside it. For two hours, they went through the albums. Some of the photos depicted Sinead Gleason's life before she met Jim Mollenkopf. She'd grown up in Boston; her father was one of thirty-six thousand gunners trained at the Kingman Army Air Field during World War II, and he had returned there to operate heavy construction machinery after the war. Sinead was twenty when the older but dashing auto repair shop owner courted her in 1948, twenty-two when her only child was born, twenty-eight when the shard from the propane explosion took her away.

The photos of their little family showed a tall red-haired woman and her lookalike daughter doing the things mothers and daughters did on vacations. The pride of the husband behind the camera was palpable through the old black and whites.

"Things would have been different if Mom hadn't gotten killed, don't you think?" Siobhan said.

Her father didn't respond. She saw that he had taken out his hearing aid and fallen asleep sitting in his bed. The binder was open in his lap. He was smiling.

She decided to let him sleep. She was tired herself. She headed to her bedroom, through the living room, but paused when she saw his computer. She wondered what someone like her dad would find so engrossing.

The screen was sleeping, but when she touched the space bar, it awakened. She saw that her father had been visiting an online network not that different in format from the Grapevine. When she looked more closely, she could see it was called LibertyNet. Her father had clicked to a discussion called *Patriots Blamed for Murder— Wish It Were True*.

She checked on her father, who was still sound asleep, and returned to the screen. The system had logged her father out, but she could scroll backward through the discussion. People with handles like *JohnBirchLives* and *Armageddon* and, on several occasions, *Kingman* argued that this Spider character had a hell of a nerve, going on the radio and spreading the Jew lies of the ZOG Secret Service. Someone ought to teach him a lesson, was the discussion's consensus. The dial-in number for the network was in the header at the top of the page, and Siobhan copied it into her notebook.

It was still just nine o'clock. The only phone she had seen in the house was on the nightstand next to her dad's bed. She drove back to the Amoco station. She'd tell her dad she had a sudden notion to see Kingman at night, if he asked.

Spider picked up on the second ring. "What a welcome surprise," he said. "Are you at SFO?" He sounded to Siobhan like he'd had a couple.

"I'm in Kingman," she said. "With my dad."

"Oh," he said. "How is that?"

"Mixed," she said. "He's being super sweet to me."

"But," Spider said.

"But he's still an over-the-top right-winger, and now he's on some computer network where people are talking about hurting you because you went on the radio to talk about Yosh."

"That's why you called?"

"Spider," she said. "These people..." She didn't know how to finish the thought.

"Okay," Spider said.

"Okay?" she said. "What does that mean?"

"You want me to be careful, right?" he said. "That's why you called. I'll be careful. That's what okay means."

She was worried her dad might wake up and wonder where she was. "Okay," she said, "I've got to go now, before my dad realizes I'm gone. Please be careful. These people are nuts."

When she got back, her dad was still asleep. She dozed fitfully, wanting to be gone. In the morning, her dad made a big thing of taking her to IHOP for blueberry waffle pancakes with vanilla ice cream, her childhood favorite. It was hard to connect the doting old man across the table with the threatening messages on LibertyNet.

"Did Mom agree with you about political stuff, Dad?" she said, more to break the silence than anything. "I know you have strong feelings."

He colored slightly. "She did not, as a matter of fact," he said. "We disagreed about everything. People called us Ralph and Alice, like on *The Honeymooners*. She was a Gleason, you know. We would go at it, we would make our points, but we didn't let it interfere with what we had." He seemed lost in happy memories.

When it was time for her to go, he hugged her for a long time. She thought he was going to start crying again, but he kept it together.

"Go," he finally said. "Don't wait so long next time."

Chapter 21

WHEN SIOBHAN HAD TOLD HIM OF HER PLANS to take a solo trip, Spider grunted that he understood, but he didn't really. All he understood was that she'd done it again. He was an idiot.

It was like the scorpion and the frog. He was her faithful frog. It was her nature. There was a reason she was single. She hadn't found anyone in New York, so now she had reclaimed and then renounced Spider, breaking her own previous land speed record in the process.

There was a reason he was single too. Her.

It was time to move on.

He had a bottle of twelve-year-old Macallan's for special occasions, and this was special all right. He wondered if this trip of hers wasn't really about rekindling with Mel in New York. Her stated reason was that something had come up at work. And then she made a special point of adding that she needed time to be by herself, that it was going too fast between them.

Too fast! Ten years!

He poured himself another. Then she called back, to warn him about the computer goblins. His good buddy, looking out for his interests. The hell with that. He had another tot.

He was hungry. He didn't feel like defrosting anything. He took a shower to clear his head and set out for the Caffe Sport in North Beach. The hushpuppy felt snug in the duster pocket. He supposed he could give Schollmeyer as a reference if for some reason he were stopped.

The Caffe Sport had two claims to fame: a salad featuring squid marinated in near emetic amounts of garlic, and waiters who served customers contemptuously. Consequently, the restaurant enjoyed a large cult following.

It was not easy to find a place in North Beach to park, even late on a weekday evening. He circled the Sport, moving progressively higher up Telegraph Hill, away from the restaurants and night life. On upper Green, just before Montgomery, he finally found a space big enough for the Citroën.

The Sport was four blocks down a steep cobblestoned hill from his parking space. The street was ill lit, but there was a steady stream of folks from the apartment buildings that overlooked the Bay descending with Spider toward food and entertainment in North Beach or Chinatown.

Spider took a seat at the Sport's counter. The counterman made eye contact, Spider nodded, and a squid salad materialized. It took two glasses of wine and the better part of a third to hold the garlic to a draw. He was feeling a bit better now.

A heavy black voice said "Fo' Fo' Fo'" behind him, and he felt better still. He liked Garland Young.

Garland and Spider always greeted each other the same way, an homage to their first, chance meeting in a Mission District bar during the NBA title series a few years back. Moses Malone had accurately predicted three four-game sweeps for his Seventy-Sixers. For a while, Spider and Garland cut a swath through the SF social scene. "Fo' Fo' Fo'" became their battle cry—four bars, four parties, four drinks, four joints, four lines. Once, four girls, but Spider didn't like that very much.

It was accepted amongst Garland's friends that he emphasized the ghetto in his speech by choice; he was from a middle-class background in Atlanta and held a Stanford Master's in urban planning.

"Fo' Fo' Fo'," Spider replied. "How the fuck are you?"

"They have fit me with a bridle," Garland said, "and come Monday, I am going to have to wear it."

"Or as we say in our language?"

Garland said he was starting a full-time gig as a fundraiser for Stanford. "We're going for five hundred million bucks," he said, "to better educate the rich." He shook his head in wonder at his career evolution. "Come meet my fiancée," he said. "You hitched yet?"

"It's a sad story," Spider said. He provided the highlights as he settled his counter bill.

"Would it offend you if I said I see a pattern here?" Garland said.

"Deeply. Actually, no. Even I can see it."

At Garland's table, two nice-looking women smiled up at them. Garland introduced his fiancée, Veronique, short and sleek, with a French accent and a head like an afghan hound's. She was his boss at Stanford, as well as his betrothed.

Her equally svelte friend, Anne, was smoking a Carleton with reckless abandon. She worked for Fitzgerald, Vaughan, and Clooney, a local marketing firm. Various jokes about female singers were shared, tunes were hummed, lyrics quoted. Some incidental touching took place. It was fun. Red wine flowed.

A small furor from across the room rose above the restaurant's hubbub. Two husky bearded men with hair in bandanas were vocally upset. There was nothing unusual about seeing such men in a North

Beach restaurant or anywhere else; they might be poets, fresh from a reading at City Lights.

It was clear these particular poets had objected to the waiter's high-handedness. The waiter was bowing and scraping, overly obsequious. "Yes, sir," he trilled, so the whole restaurant could hear. "Spaghetti carbonara with double extra bacon, on its way."

The waiter shuffled the phlegm in his throat conspicuously as he headed back toward the kitchen. Diners tittered, and the bearded men looked around suspiciously.

Spider needed to piss. Over the stall, the graffiti said, MY MOTHER MADE ME A HOMOSEXUAL; GIVE HER SOME WOOL AND SHE'LL MAKE YOU ONE TOO.

When Spider left the bathroom, one of the poets was waiting outside. The passage was narrow and both men were thick, so the waiting man had to press himself into a wall to allow Spider's exit.

As dictated by etiquette, Spider didn't make eye contact. Instead, he focused on the elaborate tats displayed on the man's biceps. The designs were intricate and, at quick regard, seemed to overflow with motorcycles and lightning bolts, surrounded by letters, numbers, and runes. There was a single vivid spot of color, a teardrop in dark red, in the center of each black ink tat.

Back at the table, Garland and the women were engrossed in the TV above the bar. The newscaster informed them that the Supreme Court had ruled the state of Georgia was within its rights in outlawing sodomy.

"When sodomy is outlawed, only outlaws will get blowjobs," Garland said, and the women giggled. Anne threw a napkin at Garland, and he snapped for it like a trained seal.

The trajectory of the evening was assuming familiar dimensions. Garland would know somewhere great to go. Spider was leaning toward going where Garland led, but Anne said she had an early yoga class.

There was a time when he would have asked her what she was doing for breakfast. He had learned that some women found this very sexy, sort of like a trial run to find out what a guy would be like in the morning. This time they all exchanged bibulous embraces, and then Garland and the two women moved away from Spider, toward Garland's car, parked in the Vallejo Garage. Spider trudged up Green toward the DS, reflecting that he should grow up and start parking in garages.

Green was deserted now. Beyond Grant, little lanes cut in, and then Kearny Street and then a very dark block of Green, just before his car. It was colder now, too. He was glad to be wearing the duster.

Two motorcycles coasting up the hill behind him suddenly stopped and cut their lights. One was a few feet in front of him, the other an equal length in back. The riders jumped off and rushed him.

Spider reached for the hushpuppy as one of the men made a spinning motion with his hand. Spider felt his right ankle pulled off the ground by the nunchuck. He fell on his stomach, and one of the men drove his boot between Spider's leg into his testicles.

The kick launched him forward, faint with pain. The men stood over him laughing.

His arms had splayed in front of him when he fell. His head still mashed into the pavement, he felt in his pocket for the little gun. He thought he could roll over and fire, but he underestimated the pain. He rolled just far enough to get off a misaimed shot in the general direction of the laughter, and then had to roll back on his stomach.

He heard the unique burp of the silencer, but he didn't hear any cry of pain. He was steeling himself to be kicked again when he heard the sound of engines revving and motorcycles taking off.

Spider had gotten the briefest of looks when they charged him. They might be the guys from the Sport, he thought, but he couldn't swear to it. It had happened very quickly.

The man had taken close aim with a heavy boot and given it all he had. Spider had been kneed in the groin infinite times playing basketball, but this pain was of a different order entirely. It felt like something was broken. After a quarter hour, someone walked by, and Spider got him to call an ambulance.

At the hospital, a doctor poked around, causing Spider to scream. The doctor said they would have to probe inside, and the sooner the better. Was he okay with anesthesia and whom should they notify?

Spider gave them Ohanian's number and then gratefully let the anesthetic do its thing.

Chapter 22

Ukiah, Sunday, July 7

"A Call To Patriots."

Cal Albright looked critically at the words, which he'd just inscribed in careful capitals on a legal pad. It was the latest in a series of attempts at a headline.

"Stand Up And Be Counted."

"The Time Is Now."

"Now Is the Time."

"Don't Tread On Me."

"A Land of Our Own."

"The White Bastion Needs You."

"Hear the White Bastion's Call."

"Heed the Call of the Bastion."

"A Haven for White Families."

He didn't feel sure about any of them. He was trying to create an ad for Reverend Footman's newsletter, to issue a call without showing his hand to the ZOG.

He couldn't get past the headline. Each one seemed worse than the one before. Ernie Fresser was pretty good at things like this, but Cal had had it with Ernie Fresser.

Cal was disgusted, too, with Reverend Joseph Footman, who had accepted Cal's huge tithe but reneged on his commitment to be an active partner. Instead, Footman had poured himself into the counterfeiting project, personally handing out packets of twenties to trusted confederates and monitoring their progress in passing the bills.

Cal debated whether to aim his ad at recruiting single men or family men. Men without families were loose cannons, but family men didn't like to take risks.

Cal looked at his headlines one more time and decided to take a break. He turned to a fresh page on the pad and began writing a coded message to his soldiers to say he wanted to know once and for all who was in and who was out on the Ngvotpss job.

Ngvotpss was Missoula, of course, in Cal's simple but foolproof code. It annoyed the dickens out of Cal that the men complained about how hard it was to remember and decipher. They complained about a lot of things now, more than before the Brink's haul. They had all signed a blood compact, called themselves the Army of the Already Dead, sworn to face torture from the Israelis to whom the ZOG would deliver them if they were ever captured. But Cal wasn't so sure about some of them now.

Most of them, actually. Odin had admitted blabbing to his girlfriend about pulling off the job. Odin told Cal she was as big a patriot as any of them and deserved to know. What they both deserved was to be executed for unauthorized secret-sharing. It was in their covenant in black and white. But Cal was pretty sure the rest of the men wouldn't have much of a stomach for an internal execution, so he just flayed Odin verbally and let it slide.

It seemed unfair that the man who had led the biggest heist in probably ever couldn't get more respect and cooperation. He was a young lion, like Pastor Jack had said, but he couldn't do it all alone.

•••

ERNIE FRESSER SWIRLED THE DREGS OF HIS BOURBON on the rocks. He had gone to the No Man's Land bar on the Rez to be by himself and think things through.

The more he drank, the darker he thought. He had a lot to think about. Cal, for example, his leader and friend, who had turned so sour and critical. No one told Ernie Fresser to keep his trap shut. He took the last swallow of his drink and banged the glass too loudly on the bar to indicate his readiness for another. Cal had a burr up his ass about the Jew getting killed. Ernie wondered who had killed him. In any case, they were set up for the reward, and they were scot-free on the blame. What was Cal's problem?

Then there was the business with Reverend Footman. The reverend had shown up unexpectedly at the prayer meeting on Friday, pulled him aside, and asked if he was up for a special mission. With the reverend asking, the answer had of course been yes, even before Footman told him the nature of the mission.

Ernie reflexively checked that his wallet was in his side pocket per usual. The wallet contained forty twenty-dollar bills freshly minted at Ararat. The reverend told him they were flawless. He wanted Ernie to pass two hundred of them. The rest of Ernie's bills were in the closet where he kept his Aryan lore.

It took a long time to pass twenties. You had to find a lot of places where you could make small purchases and get change. You couldn't buy a cup of coffee at the same Circle K six times a day.

Ernie had passed twenty-nine bills in six days. After subtracting the cost of the coffees, packs of gum, newspapers and sundries, he had accumulated $522.46 for the movement. Footman had said he could keep ten percent. The whole thing seemed like the smallest of potatoes compared to what they'd taken off the truck.

"Well, look who's here," said a voice in his ear. "If it ain't Deputy Dawg hisself."

The smartass longhair reporter from the paper, the one who had covered the public meeting and his dismissal, made himself at home on the adjoining barstool. He had on his hangdog corduroy jacket, and his blue work shirt spilled out over the front of his jeans. He held up two fingers to the bartender.

"Don't you know it's bad to drink alone?" the reporter said. "Makes you crazy. Look at me." Ernie grunted and threw back his current drink when the bartender set down the new one. "You white folk ready to make your move?" the reporter said.

Ernie felt his face reddening. He could hear Cal's voice in his head: *The true agent masks himself, encourages trust, then wreaks his will.* It was hard to mask yourself with an absolute tool like this reporter. But he wouldn't give anything away. He wasn't a fool, no matter what Cal seemed to think.

"Who knows," Ernie said. "Maybe you'll be surprised. Maybe you'll wish you said we white folk, not you white folk."

"Maybe pigs will grow wings and fly out of my butt."

"Just read your own newspaper," Ernie said. "Stay informed."

"And what might I read in that newspaper?" the reporter responded.

Ernie fixed him with what he thought of as his death stare, the one he had liked to use on recalcitrant offenders.

"You look like a walrus," the reporter said. He attacked his drink. "Who am I to talk, right?"

The reporter wandered off into his own thoughts, and the two men drank in silence. Then the reporter said again, "So what might I read in that newspaper?"

"Whatever catches your eye," Ernie said. He thought it was a pretty clever answer.

"Okay, I'll play," the reporter said. "Ukiah couple achieving dream of processing wool in Mendocino County. Am I warm?" Ernie didn't dignify him with a reply. "Rocks thrown from overpass of Highway 101? That sounds about the right speed for you guys."

Ernie wanted to shake the reporter by the throat. Instead, he said, "We think a little bigger than that."

The reporter waggled two fingers and was rewarded with two more drinks. "Even bigger than that, hey?" he said. "Boggles the mind."

The reporter took a swallow. "Then I guess you robbed the Brink's truck and killed Steinmetz. You're a regular reign of terror, huh?" The thought made him laugh. "Hey, look," he said to the bartender. "I'm drinking with John Dillinger." He gave a guffaw that brought up some of his last swallow.

"That's disgusting," Ernie said. "And so are you."

The reporter didn't seem bothered. "O ho," he said. "Mr. Manners doesn't approve. So sorry. Time to put this little boy to bed." He almost fell getting off the stool and lurched out.

Ernie finished his drink and called for the tab. It was thirty-eight dollars, more than he'd expected, and he realized he was buying the reporter's drinks too. That really jacked him off. He put two of the reverend's twenties on the counter and walked out.

•••

SHERIFF GRAY WAS A BORE AND BILL RICCI Jr. was a disappointment and a constant irritant. This was the opinion of Bill Ricci Sr. as the meal wore on, with Guido the chef pulling out the stops for Gray, who was from Riverside County and in charge of the CAMP commandos in the three pot-centric counties that comprised the

Emerald Triangle. It was a courtesy call by the invading general on the local baron.

Bill Jr. had dropped by before dinner, as often happened. Ricci Sr., preoccupied, hustled the meal along, not even demanding that Guido expound on the hoary art of pounding veal to wafer-thin succulence.

"How is the campaign going, Sheriff?" Bill Jr. asked. "Made any big kills—confiscations, I mean—recently?"

"Indeed, we have," the sheriff said. "By the end of this growing season, we'll rip right through a million pounds taken off the market. Here's something that might surprise you. The armaments. We've gathered upward of two hundred unregistered, potentially lethal weapons and booby traps."

"You missed one automatic meat grinder, from what I heard," Bill Jr. said.

The comment cheered his father a little. "A damn good thing that you did, hey?" he said.

"Well," the sheriff said. "I don't condone murder." He made a jokingly stern face and wagged a finger at the other two men. Bill Jr. laughed loudly.

"I talked with Sheriff Cassidy, you know, the local guy," Gray said. "He said his people thought it was a pot deal gone bad. Now some Secret Service special agent's turned up talking about white power crazies."

Bill Jr. said, "Secret Service special agent! Wow. We've made the big time."

His father shot him an annoyed glance and pondered the new information. Albright was one of those crazies, all right, with his harebrained bastion talk. He must have left his scent on the job somehow, though why the Secret Service would get involved was a puzzler. It was a good thing he hadn't paid him off.

"What brings this special agent to suspect these white supremacist characters, I wonder?" he said to Sheriff Gray.

"Yeah, me too," said Gray. "Sheriff Cassidy said it was something about the weapon."

"Dad wants to give a medal to whoever did it," Bill Jr. said. "I'd of done it myself, and I'm practically a pacifist."

Bill Jr.'s own son—Bill III, or Threbil as he was known to the family—had been assailed by a schoolmate who told him his gramps was a sociopath. Threbil said no one could get away calling Grandpapa names, so the kid pushed him into the gravel, where he suffered a lacerated elbow. Threbil asked his mom what a sociopath was and received still another ad hoc vocabulary lesson; she had previously been forced to explain to him the meanings of "dickwad" and "scumbag," and why the words were inappropriately applied to Grandpapa.

"But you didn't," the sheriff said. "Nor did your father, who was repeatedly subjected to such immense defamation."

"To the dearly departed," Bill Jr. said, gaily waving his glass, sloshing red wine on the white tablecloth.

Chapter 23

Bisbee, Arizona, and Alamogordo, New Mexico
Saturday, July 6, to Sunday, July 7

SIOBHAN REACHED THE COPPER QUEEN HOTEL IN BISBEE at three, checked in, and went down to the bar to meet her clients. On the television screen, twenty-two robust young men pursued college football bragging rights for the state of Georgia. Drinking beer at tables in front of the TV were another ten men who mixed chemicals in a plant outside of town. Two of them had tested sterile; most of the others hadn't yet agreed to be tested.

Bisbee had been a Phelps-Dodge copper mining town since the first vein was discovered in 1880. The most notable event in its history had occurred in 1917, when two thousand vigilantes deputized by Phelps-Dodge solved the company's labor problems by seizing thirteen hundred IWW mineworkers and their supporters, loading them into twenty-three manure-filled cattle cars, and depositing them two hundred miles away, in Tres Hermanas, New Mexico, penniless and without food or water. If they returned to Bisbee, the Wobblies were told, they would be lynched.

The IWW miners never returned. The Phelps-Dodge kidnappers were never punished.

Workers represented by a pliant union worked the inexhaustible pit, weathering the Depression when copper prices bottomed. When good times returned, the mines expanded. Now, Phelps-Dodge had just closed the last, exhausted pit. There wasn't a lot of other work in Bisbee. Some outsiders were trying to turn it into a destination, a low-rent Aspen full of history. In the meantime, there was the salvage yard, the Cochise County office building, and the non-union chemical plant.

Siobhan mingled during the second half of the game. She could tell she made the men nervous. She told them she was a small-town Arizona girl herself. The Yellowjackets were beating holy hell out of the Bulldogs, but the men watched the game as if it were a nail-biter.

"Guys," said an older man, who was the law firm's main contact, "if I can have your attention." He said that Siobhan had come a long way to update them about the lawsuit and answer any questions.

Siobhan told them about the strategy to link into one action all the complaints from the various facilities that handled DBCP. The deepest pocket was Dow Chemical, which manufactured the product, so they had to build a case that Dow had ignored its own report and allowed the chemical to be widely used. "This can be huge," Siobhan said. "But it won't be quick. The key is for everyone to be tested. At the same time, we'll document what the plant owners knew all along and kept secret. You've got to be patient. You've got to stay united."

The men looked back at her with blank expressions. "It's all about filing as a class," Siobhan said. "That way we get the maximum settlement and we pressure the government and OSHA to fix the problem."

"Shit," one of the younger men said, "I don't trust the government, and I don't trust lawyers, either, no matter how pretty they are."

"Frank and Eddie," one of the other men said. These were the two workers who had already tested sterile. "They ran benzene. That's where they got it. We don't run benzene."

"You're full of shit," Siobhan's contact said. "There's benzene in hexane, and you run that every day."

"Well, we got safety stuff, we got all the fucking procedures," another man said. "We just don't take the time to do it."

"Joe does it."

"Joe's a pain in the ass."

It went on like this. It was frustrating. The men were proud of not using their allotted sick days, showing up even when suffering from one of a slew of "minor" complaints—burning hands, peeling skin, headaches, boils—lest their absence make things harder for their brother workers. They were mostly ex-miners who thrived on danger.

Siobhan said it was important to get all the evidence so that OSHA could see how things really were.

"OSHA doesn't deserve it," said the young man who didn't trust the government. All the men laughed.

The next afternoon, she drove three hundred miles east to Alamogordo, New Mexico. She arrived at her motel at nine. In the morning, she would meet workers from the local plant over breakfast.

Her motel room looked out toward the white sand dunes to the west. On those dunes, the course of human history had been changed forever when the first nuclear device was exploded on the Air Force's Alamogordo Bombing and Gunnery Range in 1945.

Siobhan had acquired a bottle of brandy, and now she settled down with it and her Kaypro. She worked on a progress memo for her office, waiting for the brandy to make her sleepy, but it didn't.

She had her modem in her bag. She thought about dialing into the Grapevine, but a wave of paranoia swept over her. She didn't want Mel to know where she was. She was pretty sure he could trace a login.

She felt wide awake. She looked up the phone number she had copied off her father's screen, connected her modem to the motel's phone line, and reached LibertyNet's login screen. It featured a drawing of a stern, muscular man, his arms crossed over his chest, and the words PATRIOTS ONLY ENTER HERE emblazoned above his head.

In the user ID box, Siobhan typed *Kingman*. For the password she typed her mother's name, *Sinead*.

The system rejected her.

Siobhan felt thwarted but also some relief. It wasn't necessarily her father who had posted in that forum about Spider; there were certainly other pinheads from Klansman, Arizona, on that absurd network.

Still, she entered *Kingman* again and then *sinead*, and the system rejected her again. Then she tried her mother's name entirely in upper case, and the welcome screen rolled back to let her in.

It was almost midnight. It was unlikely that her father was awake. Still, she felt nervous that he would log on and learn someone else was using his login. She found the discussion *Patriots Blamed for Murder—Wish It Were True*. There was one new comment, from *Kingman*: "Let's look before we leap, people. This could be a trap. This Spider fellow is likely to be under guard 24/7. We can find better targets."

Always taking care of his little girl, that nutjob dad of mine, Siobhan thought. She scrolled through the other discussions, repelled and fascinated by what she read. She paused over a discussion headed *Wish List*.

"Let's say," said the first post in the discussion, from *YoungLion,* "that we were able to take down a Brink's truck or the equivalent. How would you spend the money?"

The Patriots wished for many things. Nuclear warheads and planes to carry them. A network-strength TV station of their own. Heavy artillery of all descriptions. Vast land purchases to carve out enclaves.

Their daydreams were interrupted by another post from *YoungLion*: "Thank you for your suggestions. The event referred to netted $3.3 million. We will need a hundred times that to realize Earl Turner's vision. Will you stand up?"

Siobhan reread the post. The wording and tone seemed to suggest direct knowledge of what *YoungLion* called "the event." He sounded like he was recruiting. She continued reading. The subsequent posts deferred to *YoungLion*. People asked him how soon he thought it would be before the coffers got another boost. *YoungLion* said, "Planning is continuous."

Half a dozen posters said they wanted to stand up. Siobhan assumed that these conversations continued somewhere else.

Siobhan wondered if Spider's contact at the Secret Service knew about the network. Of course he did, she thought. She herself had stumbled on it, but the Secret Service, with all its resources, was undoubtedly on the case.

She wondered what the law said about privacy on these new networks. It wasn't her branch of the law.

Eventually, she broke the LibertyNet connection. The brandy was starting to work. She dozed briefly and then started awake. Her mind wouldn't shut up. She thought about calling Spider, to tell him about what she'd just read on LibertyNet, but then she remembered how he had reacted to her last call. Obviously, he was mad at her. A late-night call would be too loaded, she thought; she would call him in the morning.

Instead, and against her better judgment, she dialed the familiar number and logged onto the Grapevine. Everything was normal. There was a friendly email from Isabel containing office gossip and an inquiry about her trip. There was a sysop message from Mel providing the system's downtime schedule for the next month.

She thought about Mel and Spider and taking a break from men. She shouldn't lump Mel and Spider together, she thought, but she did anyway. On her second motel cup of brandy, both relationships seemed to have a similar unreality. How could she have been so wrong about Mel? She had been horny, was the reason, and he was different than the other New York guys she had dated.

As for Spider, Isabel was right. Siobhan could see that clearly now, studying the amber liquid in the plastic cup. When momentous events occur, hormones snap to attention. Isabel said there were books written about STS, Shared Trauma Survival. People ended up hating each other, because the trauma was all they had in common. It wasn't something to build a life on.

It was hard but good to be alone in this motel room having these thoughts, she thought. Her perspective was returning. She would find a new and better job in New York and meet a good man. Women were having kids into their forties now. She didn't have to panic.

Chapter 24

San Francisco, Saturday, July 6, to Monday, July 8

"THERE IS NOTHING BROKEN. YOU ARE ONE LUCKY guy," the Sikh doctor told Spider on Saturday morning, after a night in the hospital. "A quarter inch to the left, and no more little…" The doctor looked at the chart to remind him of the patient's name. "Arachnids."

Spider forced a smile. The doctor was in a good mood. He told Spider he'd get away with massive swelling and a lot of pain that would recede over time. He was free to move around as much as he could tolerate. He could have sex when he could stand it. "If she's very pretty, okay," the doctor said. "Otherwise, maybe wait a while."

Ohanian fetched him from the hospital at two. The hospital equipped him with a vial of Percocets and instructions to avoid alcohol, lest it potentiate the painkillers. "What does potentiate mean?" Spider asked Ohanian.

"It's a pharma weasel word," Ohanian said. "So loaded patients don't get into car accidents and sue their ass."

Spider took his pain pills with scotch and soda and fell into a deep, wonderful sleep. When he awoke, it was dark, and there was a note from Ohanian saying there was a turkey sandwich in the fridge and he would be back in the morning.

Every movement was an effort. He ate the sandwich, gulped another Percocet, potentiated, and turned on the TV. It was the ninth day of the Tour de France, and the camera followed the bicycle riders on their foggy, hilly journey from Strasbourg to Ëpinal. It was a sport that meant nothing to Spider, yet he found the coverage deeply engrossing, so much so that he fell asleep five minutes in.

When he awoke, it was midmorning Sunday, and Ohanian was drinking coffee and smoking a joint at the kitchen table. Ohanian picked up the phone and put it on the bedside table. "In case there's someone you want to call," he said.

"Not at the moment," Spider said.

"Don't be a stubborn dog," Ohanian said. "The lady cares about you. Call her."

"Not now," Spider said. He couldn't explain it, but it was clear to him that he didn't want her to know what happened. It would come off as a pity play, and he wasn't going to do it. Especially after she'd warned him.

After Ohanian left, Spider picked up the receiver and dialed. When a voice answered, Spider said, "Fo' Fo' Fo'" in as assertive a voice as he could muster.

"Fo' Fo' Fo'," said the voice on the other end. "Whass hap'ning, my Spiderman?"

Spider told Garland Young about getting jumped and asked him exactly what he remembered about the guys in the restaurant.

"Basic bikers," Garland said. "Big tall guy, big short guy. You pissed with the short guy. Did you piss on him?"

"There was the tat," Spider said. "I'd like to find that tat."

"Good luck," Garland said. "What are you going to do? Head over to Dogpatch and tell the Pariahs to line up for inspection?"

If you'd lived in SF any time at all, you knew about the local branch of the Pariahs and their clubhouse, where Tennessee Street dead-ended in the Dogpatch neighborhood just south of downtown. Over the years, they'd become a San Francisco thing, like Tony Bennett or It's-It or Fisherman's Wharf.

"Hey!" Garland said. "Your dick going to work again?"

"They think so," Spider said. "Appreciate your concern."

Spider called Schollmeyer at his office phone, expecting to get an answering service on a Sunday, but the agent picked up on second ring. Spider told him what had happened.

"I'll be darned," Schollmeyer said. "Right there in the middle of town. They're getting frisky."

"Are you all right?" he added as an afterthought.

"I will be, eventually, it appears," Spider said.

"Tell me about the tattoos," Schollmeyer said. "Could it have been two letters, A and B, intertwined?"

Spider said he had noticed letters and numbers, but he hadn't had time to give them a good read. "What would the A and B tell you?" he asked Schollmeyer.

"Aryan Brotherhood," the agent said. "Which is what happens when you don't execute people."

He explained to Spider that the organization was led by people serving life sentences without possibility of parole and, therefore, nothing to lose. They had become the dominant and most murderous gang inside the federal penitentiaries. They befriended biker prisoners, who carried out their bidding once released back to the world.

"Could be Hell's Angels," Schollmeyer said. "Could be Bandidos. Or even Mongols. The Brotherhood has its hooks into all of them now. Could you pick the guy out of a lineup?" He sounded buoyant.

"I know it doesn't make your testicles feel better, but this could be a big break."

"Always glad to be helpful," Spider said. "I don't know about the lineup, though. I got a really quick look at one guy at the restaurant. If it's even the same guy. And an even quicker look when they jumped me."

Schollmeyer cleared his throat. "So, since I got you on the line, did you get any response to that call for leads?"

Spider found it difficult to evaluate the information he had received from his callers. They had remembered numerous arguments with right-wingers of one stripe or another. None of the arguments seemed more or less likely to result in someone picking up an automatic weapon and pulverizing Yosh on a back road.

"Yeah," Spider said. "A lot of response, but nothing, you know, jumping out."

"Well, the next call could be the one," the agent said. "You never know. It's good to make 'em jumpy."

"Really good," Spider said.

•••

OHANIAN CAME BY AGAIN IN THE EVENING, AND they discussed Schollmeyer's theory. Ohanian said it was the only explanation that made sense, other than the North Beach attack being totally random. Spider thought you couldn't really rule out random. So much of his life had been.

In the night, the pain subsided. For stretches, he felt almost like himself. In the morning, the phone rang. "Spider," Siobhan said, "How are you. I'm on to something."

He thought a moment about what to tell her and then said, "I'm fine. What's up?"

"You know that white power computer net I told you about? The one my dad's on? I think they pulled off that armored car robbery and they're planning more."

"They?"

"People there. They talk about it like they did it. You ought to tell that agent. I expect he already knows, but just in case."

She told him in detail what she'd read.

"All right," he said. "I'll call Schollmeyer."

"Everything okay?"

"Tickety-boo," he said.

"Let me know what the agent says. Take care."

Not even an "I miss you." When he hung up, he thought of calling Schollmeyer but decided it could wait. Instead, he put the hushpuppy in the duster coat pocket and walked gingerly to the garage, leaning on the ebony-pommeled cane that Ohanian had loaned him.

Mikael was overseeing three apprentices from Mission High School, who were tuning a boxy Volvo 142S. Spider clumped to his Citroën corner of the garage, trying to avoid Mikael's view, which was impossible. The Swede raised his eyebrows at Spider across the apprentice's bent backs. Spider mimed a basketball shot with his free hand and then cupped his groin and grimaced. Mikael rolled his eyes and returned to invigilating the apprentices. Mikael considered himself a steward of the Volvo brand, and he expected his apprentices to feel the same.

Volvos were all right in their sedate way, in Spider's opinion, but couldn't hold a candle to Citroëns. In Arizona, after Viet Nam, Spider had fallen in love with the French car's looks, its exaltation of form. Compared to the cars of its time, it looked like an alien spaceship. It was all about high-speed air flow, which demanded a low, long feminine nose, a teardrop profile, and a cute behind. It was very much a guy thing. The car's name, DS, was itself a pun on the French word for goddess. By contrast, the Swedes named their Volvos after three-digit numbers.

Spider peered at the 1975 DS whose engine he was disassembling. That was the year the last DS was manufactured, before Citroën tried to improve upon perfection with a variety of even more upscale models using Maserati engines. There were twenty-one steps in removing a DS engine, and Spider was up to number sixteen, freeing the transmission shafts from the swivel bearings. He didn't really intend to work in his condition, but without giving it a lot of thought he released the handbrake cables and then removed the water header tank and the earth cable from the hoisting bracket.

His groin complained. Spider pushed through the pain. He had the Percocets in his pocket, but he wanted to stay alert.

Mikael had finished passing on his gospel and now made his way to Spider's corner. "Spare me the basketball nonsense," he said. "You got jumped. Ohanian told me. Go to bed. Now."

"Leave me alone," Spider said. An idea had been forming ever since his conversation with Garland, and he was going to run with it. "I'm fine," he said. "See?" He motioned at the water tank he'd removed.

Mikael looked dubious.

"Ohanian's an old woman," Spider said. "Prone to exaggeration. I'm going to finish here and then run some errands. Go back to your boxes."

•••

The Pariahs' house was at the very end of the cul-de-sac. They treated the street in front of their house as a parlor. For some reason, the two houses on either side of the Pariah house had proven unrentable.

DANIEL BEN-HORIN

Spider parked in the parlor and leaned out his window. Several bikers lounging about looked up at him with annoyed expressions.

"This is kind of like a private street," said a Pariah who shambled toward Spider's car.

"I've just got a question," Spider said. Two other Pariahs joined the first. All three men folded their arms across their chest. They looked like a movie poster. Spider gripped the barrel of the gun in his pocket. "I'm trying to find a guy," he said. "With bicep tats that have a red teardrop in the center. You know any gang with tattoos like that?"

The bikers looked at each other and then, wordlessly, advanced closer. Spider prepared to fishtail away. It wasn't going as he had hoped.

Then another Pariah rushed out of the house, shouting, "Hold on!" The three menacing Pariahs stopped. Spider couldn't see his tats, but from his blocky build and way of moving, the new guy looked like he might be the shorter guy in the restaurant.

The new Pariah approached Spider's car and said, "Was that a fucking hushpuppy you shot at me?"

"You got that right," Spider said. "Where were you?"

"Dak To, Con Thien, and Hamburger Hill," the Pariah said. "What about you?"

"Con Thien, Khe Sanh, and Hamburger," Spider said. "Then two months getting stitched up at Camp Lejeune. Won the gun off a SEAL playing poker in the hospital."

"Fuck me," the Pariah said. "You were at Hamburger. What unit?"

"Combat medic with the fifth Cav," Spider said.

"Fuck me," the Pariah said. "One hundred and first Airborne, me." He thought a moment. "I'll never get over what those scumbags did to us."

Spider knew he didn't mean the Viet Cong. He meant the brass who had ordered the fifth, the one hundred and first, and the ninth Marine Regiment to withdraw from Hamburger Hill after taking it with massive loss of life. The brass thought it was too risky to secure the terrain, but for the soldiers, it was a kick in the gut.

The Pariah looked at Spider appraisingly, and then said, "I'm Shorty. Come in and get high. Bring the gun."

Spider considered saying he was not currently armed. Instead, he parked the car and got out, holding the hushpuppy in front of him, the barrel and its silencer pointing down.

Shorty extended his hand, and Spider gave him the gun. Shorty examined it and then put the barrel to the head of the Pariah standing next to him and belched. Everyone laughed.

Inside, they passed the gun around, marveling at its diminutive size. Shorty showed Spider the Pariahs' collection of silencers, bulky things.

While the gun got stroked, Spider, Shorty, and the two other Pariahs who'd fought in Nam swapped stories. The Pariahs' coke and weed were top shelf. The conversation veered into reminiscences about fights and sex and righteous defense against law enforcement. The Pariahs told good stories.

It was amazing how quickly time could pass with the right substances. The sun, which was directly overhead when Spider arrived, was already on the far side of Potrero Hill, sinking toward the Pacific.

"Shorty," Spider said, in the warm glow of newfound camaraderie, "don't you like garlic? What's your problem with me?"

"Oh, yeah," Shorty said. "Sorry about that. I was just doing a guy a favor. Something about a chick. They told me you were yuppie scum."

"That what I look like?" Spider said. "Yuppie scum? Yuppie scum from Hamburger Hill?"

"Said I'm sorry. Someone gave me some wrong dope. I'll deal with it."

"It's time, man," said a Pariah who had just come into the room.

The remark galvanized Shorty. "Mongol started coming to one of our bars," he said to Spider. "We got to have a little conversation. Want to come?"

"I would," Spider said, reclaiming his gun from where it sat amidst empties and roaches on a coffee table. "But someone kicked my nuts in, and I don't move so well right now."

"I just told you I'd deal with it." Shorty carefully wrapped a tire chain around his forearm. "You're not a rent-gauging landlord, are you?"

"No." He rented out the second flat in his building at slightly below market rate, but he didn't think Shorty was looking for a detailed accounting.

The other Pariahs were in a hurry to go. "Come back tomorrow," Shorty said. "We'll get high."

Chapter 25

Ukiah, Saturday, July 6, to Tuesday, July 9

THE DAY AFTER HER DOCTOR'S APPOINTMENT, JULIE FELT mixed emotions. On the one hand, she'd been handed a death sentence. On the other hand—Esteban. He traveled with his own coffee; each morning, he brought her cappuccino in bed. He had a tongue like a furry anteater and he fucked her warmly, not like she was made out of glass. She didn't feel like she was dying when she was in bed with him.

On Saturday, an old pickup clattered into the front yard. Esteban looked out the window and said to Julie, "Finally. It is the boy, Randy. You know what to do."

When Esteban had first arrived at Yosh's in his handyman truck, he had immediately gone down into the basement. "I've always wanted to see this," he told Julie. "We were friends, Yosh and me, but he was very private about this stuff."

He had returned upstairs shaking his head. "Quite a scientist, our amigo. We're going to need an interpreter. He had a kid who worked with him a lot—Randy. Let's hope he shows up."

She herself had no clue about the operation. She couldn't even get into the basement; the stairs were too steep for her to navigate.

"What if the wrong kind of someone shows up?" Julie asked. "You know, like an heir? Wants the house. Wonders what we're doing here."

"We are Yosh's dear friends," Esteban said. "Which is only the truth. We are guarding the premises. But maybe no one like that comes. Maybe there's no will. We'll just wait and see."

Julie thought he was probably right about there not being a will. She didn't have a will. She doubted Yosh had.

Esteban said that if Randy showed up, Julie should get him to resuscitate the apparatus while Esteban himself stayed out of sight. "We've met a few times," Esteban told Julie. "He's just a kid. I think he saw me as some kind of threat from deep, dark Colombia."

"Why should he trust me?" Julie said

"Don't worry," Esteban said. "He'll go weak in the knees."

Esteban was right about that. Randy's eyes went wide when Julie opened the door to his knock. She invited him in, gave him a nice smile, and asked him if he wanted some tea.

"It's okay," he said, "I'm fine."

"Well, I'm going to have some," Julie said, "and you'll be polite and join me, right? I'm Julie."

"Randy," he said.

"Yosh was an old dear friend," Julie said while she prepared the tea. "How do you know him?"

"Well," Randy said, and then ran out of steam.

"We can be honest with each other, I think," Julie said. "I helped Yosh sell what he grew. What did you do?"

"I was, like, his technical staff. You need a lot of math to figure out the lighting and the nutrients. It's super important."

"I bet it is," Julie said. "So what are you going to do now, with all that know-how?"

The boy looked miserable. "I don't know," he said. "Yosh was like my only guy."

"So maybe you need another guy, or maybe gal?" Julie said. "Would you like a new partner? Like me?"

"Oh, god," the boy said.

"Does that mean yes?" Julie asked. "Don't keep a girl in suspense."

"Oh, god. Yes."

They had a good time that first day, Julie and Randy. He bounded up and down the stairs like a collie, renewing his acquaintance with the ladies in the basement and then finding Julie in the house, so he could explain the difference between fluorescent and metal halide lights and why it was important to swap in the halides at the end of flowering to increase potency. It was more detail than Julie needed, but she let him talk.

"You should hang out with us," Julie said to Esteban, who was hunkering in the bedroom. "He's a treasure trove. And a hoot."

"Ah no," Esteban said. "Let me be your little secret, okay? He will work harder if he has you to himself."

On Sunday, Randy showed up with a big shopping bag filled with bottles of vinegar and boxes of baking soda. He would mix them, he told her, to release carbon dioxide. "Photosynthesis, you know," he said gravely.

Randy brought upstairs a tiny seedling and a fat bud, to show Julie the beginning and end of the process. "These here are the cotyledons," he said, pointing at the two emerging leaves on the seedling. "And this is what it grows up to be."

The bud seemed to be covered with white crystals; it fluoresced and sparkled under the light. "Trichomes," Randy said. "What gets you high."

He had a magnifying glass, and he showed her how the trichomes stood like erect little soldiers, each with a cap that looked like the glans of a penis, so full it was likely to burst. "On the plant, a bud like this just pulses," he said. "I shit you not."

Randy said it was a good thing he had set up the plants' nutrients and water on a timer, or they would have been goners. As it was, they needed some major TLC, and he puttered furiously all day. When he came upstairs in the early evening, he said, "I have righted the ship."

"That calls for a celebration," Julie said, and extended to him the tray of Esteban's coke she had been on the point of sampling.

Randy's eyes lit up. "Ahh," he said, after hoovering a thick line into each nostril. "Now you're talking. This shit is as good as the Colombian flake Yosh had."

Later, Esteban said he didn't like Julie treating Randy to the coke. "It's for us," he said.

"Ah, *caro*," Julie said lightly. "You have plenty, no?"

"It's not that."

"What then?"

Esteban took a while to answer. "It is about relations," he finally said. "We must keep the right relations with Randy. He is not our partner."

"Of course not," Julie said. "But he is very helpful. Think of the coke as a productivity tool." Esteban seemed about to retort, but she glided her chair toward him, put her hand on his thigh, and said, "Speaking of which, I am feeling very productive, how about you?"

On Monday, Randy stopped by after school. He sang while he worked downstairs, mostly Bruce Springsteen songs. There would be no retreat for him, he bellowed out, and no surrender. Periodically, he interrupted his labors to sprint upstairs to show Julie something and ask if she needed anything.

She had a line ready for him each time he emerged, and he started coming upstairs even more frequently. They talked about how much he hated school and how girls didn't like him and how he wanted to make a lot of money and build a mansion in the woods.

She joined him snorting the coke more often than not. Coke was hell on her immune system, but she enjoyed hearing the teen rattle on and didn't really feel she had a lot to lose.

Esteban stayed in the bedroom as Julie and the boy discussed the foibles of teenage girls in the living room. When Julie came into the bedroom, Esteban advanced on her with carnal intent, but she pushed him away. She had told Randy she would get him some aluminum foil so he could set up a negative ion generator and dispel dust particles from the air in the basement.

"Oh, little Señor Randy," Esteban said. "I think you are in love with him."

"A little bit, but I prefer grown men," Julie said. "Still, he is our meal ticket."

"Yes," Esteban said. "When will we have some buds I can ship?"

"Soon, he says," she said. "Just sit tight, Lone Ranger."

"I am going a little crazy here, my beautiful Tonta," he said.

•••

ON TUESDAY, RANDY LEFT AT EIGHT. ESTEBAN MATERIALIZED soon after to prepare "our national dish! Bandeja Paisa!"—he had been talking about it for three days. He had his sleeves rolled up and his head in the refrigerator when Randy reappeared. "Forgot my notebook," he said as he burst through the door. He and Esteban surveyed each other.

"Hey, Randy," Esteban said. "How you doing? I'm just helping my old friend Julie out here." He turned to Julie and said, "Okay, looks like you're set. Just let me know if you need anything." He waved at Randy and went outside to his truck.

Randy was silent until they heard Esteban drive off and then he said, "I know him. What's he doing here?"

"We go back," Julie said. "He helps me out." She didn't like lying to the boy, but he was clearly upset.

"He and Yosh were tight and then they were not so tight," Randy said. "They got untight with each other a few days before Yosh got it."

"Untight how?"

"Esteban wanted to give him money and become his full partner, learn how to grow, learn the science. Yosh said no."

It made sense, Julie thought, for Esteban to want to be more than a distributor. He would only be secure if he himself were the source of the weed that guaranteed his safety.

"Yosh told you this?"

"No, I heard it. I was in the basement. It was late. They got pretty loud. Esteban said he was offering crazy money, so Yosh would be crazy not to take it, he had to take it. Yosh said he didn't have to do anything—he didn't need Esteban's money, Esteban needed to back off. Then, Esteban said it again, that Yosh was crazy, and he wasn't going to take no for an answer. Then Yosh really unloaded on him, called him a pushy, pumped-up pimp, told him to get the fuck out or Yosh would make a little phone call to someone in Cali. Yosh could really take folks down when he wanted to."

"What did Esteban say?"

"Nothing!" Randy said triumphantly. "Yosh totally shut him off. He just got quiet and left."

Julie and Randy looked at each other.

"I thought it might be him," Randy said. "But why would he kill his grower?"

"Maybe he planned to become his own grower," Julie said. The penny dropped. Esteban had needed Julie for the Randy honey pot. Suddenly, she knew she was sleeping with Yosh's murderer.

"Oh, shit," Randy said. "I'm out of here."

"Please," Julie said. "Wait. I don't want him to freak out before I can figure out how to handle this."

When Julie was stressed, her symptoms came on strong. They flooded her now. She realized her bladder was about to take a solo and pressed her thighs together to block the imminent flow.

Randy got up to leave. "See you tomorrow?" she said.

"I'm not sure," he said. "I've got to think."

Esteban returned on foot after Randy left, having stowed his truck. He had acquired a bottle of champagne, two flutes, and a bud vase with a single red rose, all of which he produced with a flourish and a suggestive smile.

"I'm sorry," Julie said. "I can't. Not tonight. I'm feeling sick. I need to be by myself."

"*Amorcita,*" he said. "I will sleep in the other room. Can I get you something?"

That Yosh's killer was a good lover and solicitous of her well-being made everything worse. She considered her alternatives. The first alternative—to confront him—was a nonstarter. He must not know she knew. He would snuff her if he thought she was a threat.

A second alternative was to kill him as he slept. She knew she couldn't do that.

What else? She needed help. She thought about who could help her. She ticked through her movement friends, all unacceptable in one way or another. Then she thought about Yosh's big friend, Spider. He had been nice enough the other day. Yosh always spoke well of him, which was quite the exception for Yosh. But she hardly knew him at all.

Julie locked her bedroom door and tried to fall asleep. At five, she picked up the phone extension in her room and dialed Directory Assistance for Spider's number. He was the only Spider Lacey in the book.

Chapter 26

"BE GRATEFUL FOR SMALL FAVORS," SECRET SERVICE AGENT Alex Schollmeyer reminded himself. It had been one of his mother's favorite adages. The small favor in this case was an irritating, very young deputy sheriff named Robertson whose assistance as a driver he had been able to secure, now that Foster had made his case on high.

"It's an incredible honor, sir," the deputy had said when they'd been introduced. His relentless good cheer was wearing Schollmeyer down. Monosyllabic replies did nothing to tamp the deputy's enthusiastic curiosity.

Two abandoned vans had been discovered in a remote nook of the forest, three weeks after the Brink's robbery. The vans had been well camouflaged; it was quite a stroke of luck that a DON'T TREAD ON ME decal, with shiny scales on the coiled serpent, had glinted in the aerial scan. The vans fit the descriptions of the vehicles the Brink's robbers had used to leave the Calpella grade.

They had run the registrations and discovered that both vans had changed hands a few days before the takedown. The previous owners lived in Santa Rosa, an hour to the south on the freeway.

Today's foray was a fishing expedition to see if either of the sellers could provide clues to the buyers. Schollmeyer assumed these had been cash transactions with bogus IDs. With luck, some physical descriptions might emerge.

"I guess you done this a ton of times," Robertson said as they pulled up in front of the house that matched the first registration. "Big holdups and all?"

Schollmeyer ignored him. The sixty-something woman who came to the door clapped her hand to her mouth when Schollmeyer identified himself.

"I certainly do," she said, when asked if she remembered the man who'd bought the van. "It wasn't him, nothing special about him. It was Liza—that's the van. We'd owned it just forever, you know. I wish I had a dollar for every scrape my boys got it in." She mused fondly over the thought. "I hated to sell it, but Sam, that's my husband, said we didn't need it anymore, so I put a sky-high price on it, eight hundred dollars, wasn't going to let it go cheap. Man didn't blink an eye."

"The buyer?" Schollmeyer said. "Anything you can tell me?"

"Better than that, I'll show you," she said. She went into another room and returned with a Polaroid photograph. It showed a tall man throwing up his hand to avoid being photographed. "I just thought it would be nice, have a photo of Liza with her new owner, but he was awful shy, said he hated photos."

The man in the photo had only partially succeeded in covering his face. "It's fucking Fresser, sir," the deputy said. "I'm sure of it."

"Sorry, ma'am," he said to the woman. To Schollmeyer, he said, "Ernie Fresser. He was a deputy. Got fired for ragging on a colored guy in a dope bust."

Schollmeyer recognized the name. Fresser was one of fifty or so regular visitors to Reverend Footman's Ararat compound. EF, he thought, and mentally scanned the list of initials in the notebook they had seized in Leclede. EF was Bunyan. He clenched his fist. They had Reverend Footman on a wiretap talking to someone code-named Earl outside of Ukiah. They had discussed Bunyan's performance. Earl wasn't happy with Bunyan. Footman counseled patience.

In the notebook, Earl was the one code name that didn't have initials next to it. He might be the key. Who was the real Earl Turner? Bunyan would know.

Schollmeyer commandeered the photo, promising to return it so they could always remember Liza. As soon as the door closed behind them, the deputy burbled about Ernie Fresser's case, the public demonstration organized by the guy who got shot up, the quick firing.

Schollmeyer took out the loose-leaf binder in which he kept the reports from the Ararat maintenance man. The cook used a five-point scale to rate where visitors stood in the hierarchy. Fresser got a two.

When Schollmeyer got back to his hotel room in Ukiah, he found a phone message from the San Francisco office. They were couriering over a still from one of the security cameras at a casino on the Indian reservation outside Ukiah. A man had paid for drinks with bills so new they squeaked, and, sure enough, they were homemade.

The courier showed up soon after. When Schollmeyer looked at the still and recognized Ernie Fresser, he whistled.

Brink's had sent him a list of all its fourteen thousand employees in the United States. Holding it, Schollmeyer felt his heart race. He held Ernie Fresser in the palm of his hand just with what he already had. Finding him on the Brink's list would be icing.

Brink's listed its employees alphabetically within the various offices. Schollmeyer started with Santa Rosa, the office closest to Ukiah. Two minutes later, he found Ernie.

Deputy Robertson was pleased to ride shotgun on the arrest. "I never liked him, sir, and that's a fact," he confided to Schollmeyer.

By seven that evening, Ernie Fresser had been booked into the Ukiah jail.

"The wheels have come off your operation," Schollmeyer told him as he turned him over to Sheriff Cassidy and left him to stew.

•••

THE PROBLEM DIDN'T LIE IN HIS ENCRYPTED COMMUNICATIONS system, Cal Albright was sure. The problem was the people he had entrusted with implementing the system.

The drill was so simple; it burned Cal up that his men couldn't master it. If you were in trouble anywhere, you found a payphone and left a message on the Kansas City machine with your code name and location. The phone monitor picked up the message. If he had to reach someone at home in order to tell them to get to a payphone, he was supposed to say, "Sorry, wrong number, I meant to call…" and then say a number, in code of course. The person receiving the call applied the code, and thus got the number of the payphone he was to call from a payphone in his own vicinity, in exactly half an hour. What could be easier?

He'd explained till he was blue in the face that home phones were poison, poison, poison. The ZOG could get your home phone records for ten years; they could find out who you called and get their phone records, and on and on, a cascade of entrapment.

So what happened? Thor had completely ignored his assignment to call the Kansas City answering machine from a payphone and relay messages as needed. Instead, Thor had called Cal at home to say that his little girl's asthma had kept him in the hospital the past three days, and he hadn't checked the Kansas City machine, could

Cal do it? Like there weren't payphones at the hospital! Cal had given him a piece of his mind.

Then, just a few minutes later, Ernie Fresser called from the Ukiah jail, in a cold sweat, saying he'd left four messages on the Kansas City machine since Monday night and here it was Tuesday afternoon, and what the hell was going on. Cal had called Ernie a dimwit and told him never, under any circumstances, to call him at home, especially from jail.

After Cal calmed down, he told Ernie to shut his mouth and keep it shut while Cal saw what he could do. First, he checked the Kansas City machine to see what other bad news he might encounter. There was Ernie's message from the night before. Ernie had actually gotten the drill right, giving his code name, saying "Ukiah jail" in code, and hanging up.

There was another message in the morning, and then two more in the afternoon, Ernie sounding more and more panicky each time, not bothering with the code. Then he'd called Cal direct.

Cal considered his options for getting Ernie a lawyer. He lacked local contacts that he could trust. He looked in his wallet, found the card he wanted, and dialed the home phone number of Richard Shelby in Pocatello, Idaho.

"Day or night," the lawyer had told him after a Council meeting. He would always be there for his kinsman.

Shelby greeted him by saying, "I'm busier than Hades. What's the emergency?"

"Bunyan's in jail," Cal said. "In Ukiah."

"How do you know it's not a DUI or a bar fight?" Shelby said.

"I don't know for sure," Cal said, "but I figure he doesn't call in unless it's an emergency." He realized as he spoke that it would be just like Fresser to call for help regardless of the circumstances.

"Well, find out and let me know. I'm up to my neck with some currency-related problems the reverend has encountered," the lawyer said.

"Wait," Cal said. "You got to find out. I can't call attention to myself right now. He already called me once at home."

There was silence from the other end. Cal wondered if the lawyer had hung up, but then Shelby said, "Here's what I can do. I've got a young fella I associate on cases in California. Smart as a whip. And committed. You got a pencil?"

Cal took down the number of a Jimmy Corr who lived in Arcata, three hours up Highway 101.

Chapter 27

SPIDER WOKE AT THREE IN THE MORNING WITH a dry throat and a pounding head. His second visit with Shorty and the Pariahs was taking its toll.

Shorty had wanted Spider to understand what made a Pariah a Pariah. He showed Spider the gang's patch, a skull with horns in the shape of motorcycle wrenches.

"Took me a year to get this, had to do some serious shit," he said. "It don't come free. But once you got it, man, it's your life." He gestured around the room. "They'd die for me, like I would for them.

"You got anyone like that?" he said to Spider. "I doubt it."

Spider thought about whom he would die for. In the war, he had almost died for people he didn't really care for. He'd taken two AK-47 slugs hauling a wounded redneck lieutenant he detested.

He supposed he'd die for his family, if he ever had one. Shorty was right; there was no one on his current to-die-for list.

"Let me tell you something," Shorty said. "We got a loyalty right here in this room and between all Pariahs everywhere that…" He paused to consider the right way to convey the enormity of it. "Man, it is just inconceivable we would betray each other. Am I right?"

He turned to the other men in the room. They were all pretty glazed by this point and just nodded their assent.

"Tell me about that scumbag," Shorty said. "The guy that set me up. He must have lied something awful to my man in New York."

"I've never met him," Spider said. "I got together with this girl I used to know in Arizona, a long time back. Next thing I know, there's a nunchuk around my ankle."

"Heh," Shorty said. "You liked that, huh?"

"He's some kind of computer nerd. That's what Siobhan— that's my girl—tells me. He's got a god thing going on. Like on this computer network, he stole Siobhan's ID and sent out bad shit under her name."

"What's a computer network?" Shorty said.

There ensued a period of the blind leading the blind as Spider attempted to explain what he didn't understand. The substances made the discourse yet more opaque.

"Okay," Shorty finally said. "I get it. This guy lied to my New York Adder brother, and I ended up doing damage to my Nam brother. A Pariah ain't ashamed to apologize. And your dick's all right, right?"

"It's the girl I'm worried about," Spider said. "She's still in New York. He could take it out on her."

"Want me to kill him?"

"No!" Spider said.

"Just yanking your chain. You want him to back off?"

"Yes," Spider said.

"I reckon I owe you," Shorty said. "Wait here." He came back with two half-pint bottles of cheap vodka. "This makes it official," he said, and threw his bottle back with a single practiced pour. There were little droplets of moisture in the outside corners of his eyes. "Now you," he said. "It's how we do it."

There hadn't seemed much of a choice at the time. Now, Spider's temples were throbbing and he was sweating profusely, though the night was cool. He took a Percocet and slept until the phone rang at six.

"Spider?" It was a woman's voice, and for a brief second he thought it was Siobhan. "It's Julie."

"Huh," he said, and then, "Hello."

"Are you okay?" she said. "You don't sound like yourself."

"I'm fine," he said. "What's up?"

"Spider," she said, "I don't have any right to ask this, and you can say no...."

Car trouble, Spider thought.

"But I don't have anywhere else to turn. And I'm very sick."

"What's going on?" he said. "Are you still in Ukiah?"

"I know who killed Yosh," she said. "He's up here in the house with me. I'm scared."

"Can you speak up?"

"I can't," she said. "He would kill me if he knew I were telling you this."

"Who is he?"

"His name's Esteban," she said. "He was Yosh's distributor— more than I was, it turns out. He tried to horn in on Yosh, Yosh said no, and he shot him."

The Secret Service agent had been so sure Yosh had been the victim of murderous Aryans. "How do you know?" Spider said.

"He wanted me to help him get Yosh's operation going again. He told me a really good story. And I...we got close. Then I found out."

"You're sure?"

Spider heard knocks on the door in Julie's room. "Okay, Mom, I love you too," Julie said and hung up.

•••

"So early on the phone?" Esteban said when she let him in. "And why the locked door, *bonboncita*?"

"I couldn't sleep," Julie said. "It's the disease. I get paranoid. I called my mom—she gets up at dawn. Please make me some tea. The fenugreek. Please hurry."

He did as he was told. When he returned, she said, "I may need a doctor. Knock on my door and check on me."

He couldn't have been nicer about it, making her toast and poached eggs at noon. "Where's Randy?" he asked at four, when Randy didn't show up as usual.

"I don't know," Julie said. "Maybe he got sick or something."

"He wouldn't call?"

"I don't know," Julie said. "I guess not."

"But your mama, she called?"

"I called her. Where is this going, Esteban?"

He was smiling as always, but it was a different smile. "Your mother's name is Spider? It is a coincidence that she has the same name as Yosh's dear friend?"

"He's my friend too," Julie said, scared. "Why are you snooping on me?" She wondered how he knew.

"It is easy to trace a call from one's own phone," he said, contemptuously reading her mind. "Your Directory Assistance is on the ball. Why did you lie about your mother?"

"To avoid this stupid conversation," she said. "Because I was afraid you'd go all jealous Latin male on me."

"You are treating me lightly," he said. "Be aware of what I am capable."

She could say, "Capable of machine-gunning Yosh," and settle it once and for all. But then he would settle her too. As for Spider, if he came up, it would be like a lamb to slaughter.

"What are we arguing about?" she said with a laugh. "I just met you. I have another boyfriend. I'm a dying woman, and I don't deny myself. Are you going to do the jealousy thing? It won't fly with me, mister, I'll tell you that right now."

He seemed to be weighing matters. "Do you have what you require?" he finally said. "Food? Drink?"

"You're sweet," she made herself say. "Maybe another cup of the fenugreek tea, with honey this time, and those little butter biscuits from Fauchon."

•••

Spider said "Julie?" then realized she had hung up. He put the receiver in its cradle and got out of bed too quickly; the spasm made him sit back down. He made himself some coffee and thought about how to get the Secret Service guy on the case.

When Schollmeyer picked up the phone at eight, Spider said, "It's Spider Lacey. I know who killed Yosh."

Schollmeyer laughed and said, "I was going to call you first thing. We got him in jail. We dug around his yard and found an Ingram Mac-10. We're getting it tested, but I'd bet my pension it's the one."

"Who?" Spider said.

"This deputy Mr. Steinmetz got fired. We got him committing about every crime in the book, including the Brink's job."

"That's not who killed Yosh," Spider said. He told Schollmeyer about Julie and what she had said about the man in the house with her.

But the Secret Service agent proved reluctant to give up his theory. "How do you know?" he asked. "The lady sounds kind of sketchy. She could be imagining things. Steinmetz was killed by an Ingram. Does this guy have one of those?"

"He could," Spider said.

"Very rare gun," the agent said. "Unlikely that he has one. And we know Fresser does."

"Can't you make a call, get a deputy up there to check out the house?"

"Make a call?" the agent said. "The sheriff up there has carefully let me know that between cleaning up after CAMP and chasing down Brink's truck leads, he really doesn't have much to offer me. I've got to use my nickel wisely with that fellow."

It was clear to Spider that the agent was only interested in Yosh's murder if an Aryan were the perp. He hung up. He thought about invoking CAMP, but that would bring a wave of rabid law enforcers to the house, with unpredictable consequences.

Spider drove reluctantly up 101. He tried to imagine different ways things might unfold, but it was a situation whose outlines he could only dimly comprehend. She was scared; that was obvious. She didn't want this Esteban to know she was talking to Spider. Had Esteban been fooled? There was no way of knowing. If he had been fooled, then Spider could be a casual old friend dropping by. But if he hadn't, if he knew Julie was calling for help, he might shoot Spider on sight. He might have already killed Julie.

He would just have to react. Spider hated the thought. This felt like so many of the Vietnam maneuvers, blind forays susceptible to ambush. There was a spectrum of possibilities, ranging from Julie being dead to Julie being fine and paranoid. She was certainly someone prone to histrionics, as her various political escapades over the years in San Francisco had made clear.

He was already in Hopland, a wide spot in the road just fifteen minutes from Ukiah. He needed a plan. Spider decided to call the house from Ukiah.

Julie answered, and he said immediately, "Are you in danger right now?"

"Yes," she said gaily. "Yes, that sounds terrific."

"I'm close by. I'm coming over unless you say not to."

"Yes," she said, "it's a lot of fun, but be careful when you go down the rapids, you don't want to drown."

She hung up. Spider considered his updated data. She was alive; she was scared; she was telling him to be careful.

It didn't really help. Spider had spent a lot of time on Yosh's property, but that had been years ago. He thought about the adjoining state park where Yosh had grown his crop in the early years. There was a main trail leading from his property into the forest, and Yosh had sited his grows off the trail, disturbing the foliage as little as possible, leaving no telltale tracks for law enforcement. Spider tried to remember if the main trail had any vehicular access.

He had a mass of topological maps in his trunk, covering most of northern California for fishing and camping purposes. He found the right topo for the forest, the one on which he had marked Yosh's house. He traced the trail from Yosh's house until it intersected a fire road about a mile from the house. The map didn't tell him anything about the condition of the fire road; it could be impossible even for a four-wheel-drive Jeep. But the DS had always risen to the occasion, and Spider decided to give it another opportunity to show its stuff.

The Citroën's suspension adjusted easily to the frequent potholes created by the last few months of rain. The road intersected the trail just where the map said it would. The trail itself was drivable for a few hundred yards but then it narrowed sharply, so Spider continued on foot.

Yosh's Better Living Through Vegetables operation had been more than a money-laundering ruse. He loved to grow things and had devoted all the land around his house to that purpose. There were a hundred yards of summer squash, basil, cucumbers, and green tomatoes between Spider and the back of the house. There was no cover at all.

If Esteban were looking out for his arrival, he'd be looking out the front. Probably. If he expected him at all. Maybe he had been taken in by Julie's charade. Spider didn't think that was the case; you'd have to be pretty dim not to hear the hysteria in Julie's voice. From where he stood on the edge of the forest, the shades on the windows in the back seemed drawn.

He could slither a hundred yards on his belly, but the prospect didn't appeal to his wounded groin. He could—what was the word?—serpentine. The movie scene popped into his mind, Peter Falk advising Alan Arkin on how to avoid bullets. It was hilarious in the movie, less so right now. Nevertheless, Falk's counsel had been sound; it is much easier to aim at someone who is proceeding in a straight line.

Spider got as low as he could and wove through the garden as if he were Joe Montana dodging pass rushers. He reached the back of the house without arousing any reaction. He was sweating and feeling foolish. Crouching low every time he passed a window, he made his way around to the front of the house. The shade of the dining room was open. He peeked in and saw Julie sitting in her wheelchair at the dining room table. There was no sign of Esteban. Julie didn't appear to be doing anything at all, just staring straight down. He reviewed the possibilities. Assuming Esteban had indeed killed Yosh, and with a vengeance, and assuming he knew of Julie's suspicions, why was he keeping her alive? Sitting there at the table, she looked like nothing so much as live bait.

He knocked on the front door and stepped to the side while he waited for it to open. Looking through the window, he could see Julie wheeling toward the door. When she opened it, he saw, over her shoulder, the man he assumed was Esteban leaning against the wall next to the back window.

"Spider!" Julie said. "What a surprise! You didn't say anything about coming up!" She was very gay. "Esteban," she said, "and now you get to meet Spider. I want you boys to behave."

The man across the room didn't move. His arms were crossed in front of his chest. Spider watched his hands, keeping his own hands at his side, the thumbs hitched into the pockets of the coat.

"I want you both to remember how sick I am," Julie caroled. She seemed hysterical to Spider. "Think of me as a shareable treasure."

"What are you doing here?" Esteban asked Spider.

"Visiting my girlfriend," Spider said. "Good to see you, babe," he added, turning his head toward Julie, and then snapping it back to keep an eye on Esteban. "Everything cool?"

"Oh, yes," Julie said. "Super. Except for the disease. It's done a number on me. I think I need to go home."

"Sure," Spider said. "I'll take you. Do you need to pack?"

Spider kept his gaze on Esteban who turned to Julie and said, "You didn't mention this, *corazón*. I would certainly drive you, no?"

"No friend like an old friend," Spider said.

"And no time like the present," Julie chirped. "I'll just grab my things." She pushed her chair toward the bedroom.

Spider and Esteban regarded each other across the room. "How's the grow going?" Spider said.

"You walked here from San Francisco?" Esteban said. "Where's your car?"

"In back," Spider said.

"In back," Esteban repeated. Esteban turned to the back window and pulled the shade apart. A half-acre of vegetables yawned in front of him. He was wearing some kind of designer sweatshirt over tight jeans. When he turned, there was a small bulge above his waist in the back. It could have been just the way the sweatshirt hung, but Spider didn't think so.

"There's a road back there," Spider said. "It's how Yosh trained me to arrive."

"It's how Yosh trained you," Esteban repeated. The corners of his mouth inched up in an ironic smile. "Like a puppy? You are big for a puppy." He looked quite cool and quite mad at the same time. Spider could see he wasn't buying it.

Esteban returned to his original position against the wall. During the long hours of waiting in Nam, soldiers practiced quick-draw moves. You had to be damn good to pull a handgun out of your ass, aim it, and fire. Spider put his hand in his pockets and tried to look nonchalant while his palm fitted itself around the hushpuppy's stock. As long as he watched Esteban's hands, he was sure he could get off the first shot.

Spider wondered what Esteban was waiting for. There was no way he could let two people who knew he'd killed Yosh walk out the door. Maybe he planned to nail them as Spider pushed Julie's chair. In any case, Spider couldn't see trundling Julie down a half-mile of trail, looking over his shoulder.

"Sort of," he said, as if Esteban's question deserved an answer. "Yosh was very particular about how things were done." Julie wheeled back into the room, a small satchel in her lap.

"Go in peace, *mi alma*," Esteban said. "I will await your return."

"Yeah," Julie said. "I'll come back as soon as I feel better." She rolled toward the front door, looking at Spider.

"Not that way," Esteban said. "His car is somewhere in the forest. The way Yosh trained him."

He seemed to Spider to be enjoying himself, thinking he held the cards, setting up his little surprise.

"Actually," Spider said. "She's not coming back. She thinks you're dangerous."

"Dangerous?" Esteban said, glancing reproachfully down at Julie. "What danger? The danger of my spilling her morning cappuccino? We are lovers. What is the danger, *querida*?"

Now he was right next to her chair, his hand on its back. When she tried to roll away, he tightened his grip, and she went nowhere. He could use her a shield, Spider realized. He might be smart enough to realize Spider wouldn't just wander in unarmed. Spider tried to imagine holding Esteban at gunpoint until the police came. He thought about the undersheriff and the huge pot grow in the basement. He badly wanted to pull out the hushpuppy and end the farce. But he couldn't do that. He tried to will Esteban to go for his gun.

"She thinks you killed Yosh," Spider said at last.

"Get out," Esteban said. He spat on the floor.

"You bet," Spider said. "We're just leaving."

Esteban released the chair and returned his hands to his side. Julie spun her chair to Spider's side. "There's just this one problem," Spider said. "I can't figure out why you would let us leave, knowing what we know."

"What do you know?"

It was a good question, Spider had to admit. All he himself knew was that Julie was sure Esteban had done it. "What do you know, Julie?" he said, watching Esteban's hands. He could feel Julie's eyes on him, trying to figure out his plan.

"You argued," Julie said. "He told you off. Randy was in the basement."

Esteban smiled. "You argue with your friends sometimes? Do you shoot them afterward? Me neither. I am civilized."

"Randy said it wasn't a friendly argument. He said you got mad and left."

"I was disappointed. I offered him a magnificent business proposition. I was surprised that he was so negative.

"And Randy?" Esteban continued. "Come on. He is permanently stoned. He has a lively imagination."

He was piling it on thick, Spider thought. Still, it was plausible. If it weren't for the bulge in the back of his pants.

"You used me," Julie said, "to get Randy working. Because you knew he wouldn't work for you after what he heard."

Spider's stomach sank. Could this be a lover's spat? A lifetime of poker-playing suggested to Spider that the other man was bluffing, but you could never be sure. Meanwhile, he needed Julie to play a stronger hand.

"That part maybe is true," Esteban said. "Sorry, chiquita, if it hurts your feelings, but you seemed to enjoy yourself. Now get out. No one is stopping you."

Julie looked at Spider, bewildered, wanting to leave. He would have to turn a card up to clue her in. "The way I see it, Julie," he said, his eyes on Esteban, "either he killed Yosh in which case he will kill us the first chance he gets, or you're paranoid. It's one or the other. And we can't leave till we know." He could tell that Esteban was getting restless with all the talk. That was good, Spider thought. "So tell us what Randy heard, Julie. No detail too small."

"He said you called Yosh crazy. Twice."

Esteban waited out her narrative with a patronizing smile.

"He said you wouldn't take no for an answer."

Esteban rolled his eyes.

"He said he would make a call to Cali."

"I knew he would not do that," Esteban said sharply. "He was just making noise."

She had drawn some blood, Spider thought. He hoped there was more.

"He called you a pushy, pumped-up pimp."

Esteban twitched. Then he smiled slightly. Spider knew the look. He'd seen it many times on the basketball court. Some guy who thought he was badder than you, holding himself in, wanting you to open your mouth and say the wrong thing so he could jump down your throat with both feet. He needed Esteban to jump, Spider thought.

Esteban said, "Are you done? We argued, yes. I killed him, no. Now go."

He just needed a little push, Spider thought. He hoped Julie had some more oil for the flames but she was silent.

"How's your mother these days, Esteban?" Spider said. He'd spent long hours listening to black soldiers in Nam play the dozens. Mostly, the snaps started with "Yo Mama." Some of them were beyond obscene. But all Spider could remember was a single funny one.

Esteban's kept his smile in place. "Get out, *maricón*," he said. He was very close to popping, Spider thought.

"Why I ask," Spider said, "is that I heard she was having financial difficulties."

Esteban stared at Spider, daring him to continue. The smile remained.

"What I heard was that she's so poor she has to do her drive-by shootings on the bus. Any truth to that?"

Esteban's smile broadened while his hand moved behind his back. Before it returned, Spider shot him in the chest. Esteban looked unbelievingly at the blood that was spreading over his golden sweater. He had a Beretta hanging from his right hand. Spider shot him again, and he pitched forward. Julie stared at Spider, her mouth agape.

"I'm glad he was going for the gun," Spider said. He looked at the body and at Julie. "You did good, lady. I'm going to go dig a hole," he said. "If I can."

He picked up a shovel and a pickax in the tool shed and set out in search of a burial plot. He would have to dig quite a hole, he thought, or the animals would sniff out the remains. The forest subsoil was rock hard and every thrust with the pickax sent a wave of pain through his body. He felt like crawling into the shallow declivity he had managed to create.

"Plan B," he told Julie, on his return to the house. He had no idea what it was, except that it started by getting the body into the trunk of the Citroën.

Esteban still lay where he had been shot, on an intricately detailed Bokhara carpet, one of Yosh's extravagances. On the wall, another acquisition, a delicate tapestry depicting the Lord Krishna surrounded by female devotees, caught Spider's eye. Yosh had bragged about it; it was valuable, the pride of his collection, gossamer thin and almost weightless. Spider took it off the wall and put it flat on the floor next to the body, which he rolled onto the tapestry. He continued until Esteban came to resemble a hastily-rolled blunt.

Spider surveyed his work. It would be hard to manipulate something so long and thin and dead. He had a better idea. "I got to get my car," he told Julie. "It will take a bit." He walked as quickly as he could down the trail and then drove out of the forest to the highway. When he got back to the house, Julie was where he had left her. Esteban too. Spider unrolled the tapestry and positioned Esteban in the middle of it. He forced the body into a seated position and pushed the torso between the legs, then used tie-downs from his car to keep the knees upright and the torso between them. Compacted in this way, Esteban was about the size of an air conditioner. Spider covered the body with the tapestry and secured it with two more tie-downs. He looped a rope through them to serve as a handle, and then bent his knees and hoisted the package into a wheelbarrow. It was painful, but not too bad; he was glad Esteban was on the small side.

He wheeled the barrow to his car and wrestled the package into the DS's trunk, eighteen cubic feet of cargo space, contoured to take advantage of the car's curves. No wasted space like in American cars.

"I feel so stupid," Julie said.

"Well, it's over with," Spider said. "You should clean up."

"I don't think anyone will come looking," Julie said. She told Spider Esteban's story.

In Esteban's suitcase, Spider found two ounces of cocaine and a passport. The picture in it was of Esteban, but under a different name. In his wallet, Spider found four driver's licenses, all with Esteban's picture and fake names.

Esteban's truck turned up nothing of note at first. Spider looked for a hidden compartment in the bed and in the cab. He opened the hood and was disappointed again, until his eye moved to the very front of the engine compartment, between the radiator fan and the front of the chassis. Citroëns managed to tuck the spare tire up there, where it served as a safety bumper, the first of its kind, but in American vehicles this was dead space. Not on this Ranger, though. There was a black metal box there that didn't serve any automotive function known to Spider. He ran his fingers around the sides of the box and found a keyhole, which matched one of the keys on Esteban's key ring. Opened, the box revealed an odd T-shaped contraption that looked like a drill. "Here's the gun that killed Yosh," Spider said to Julie. "Want to take a look?"

"No," Julie said. "Thanks." She paused. "Thanks for everything."

Spider put the gun in the Citroën trunk with its owner. He drove Esteban's truck behind the house and parked it in a copse of scrub oaks. It wasn't invisible, but you'd need to be looking for it. From what Julie had told him, no one would be searching for Esteban's truck, or Esteban either. He walked back to the front of house and got in the Citroën.

Julie sat on the porch looking calm enough. "Hang in there," he said.

Chapter 28

MEL SOMETIMES RAN WITH THE PUNKS WHO SET trash can fires in Tompkins Square Park, but that was the extent of his experience with violence. When Tramp came by on Sunday to tell him the deed had been done, Mel felt like he had ventured out on an exciting, dangerous edge. "How'd it go down?" he asked, trying to sound nonchalant, like he commissioned hits all the time.

"He's messed up, man. Believe it," Tramp said. "He's a soprano now."

Mel had invited Tramp to dinner last night to share in an orgy of canned delicacies, just past their expiry dates, gleaned from Dean and DeLuca's in Soho and complemented by clams from the Fulton Street Fish Market dumpster, most of the shells barely open. Tramp pretty much lived to eat, but he had been a no-show.

Tonight, Mel set out to make some money. He unfolded his Yamahopper moped—an underpowered little thing, but useful for finding holes in bad traffic. He could fold it up and carry it into the squat between uses.

It was eight in the evening, twilight. Mel mounted his steed and headed uptown. A Wall Street trader in a Gramercy Park loft was locked out of his computer system. This would be a profitable house call.

He hopped up First Avenue. The two bikers who had been waiting down the block from Elephant House followed him. They watched him fold up the moped outside the trader's building.

It was eleven when he came out. The trader had been effusive in his thanks and had plied Mel with farmed Sydney rock oysters, prattling about the wine. The trader was considering repaying to society some of what he had pillaged during the course of his career. Perhaps Mel would care to advise him in his future philanthropic endeavors? Mel quipped that behind every great fortune lies a great crime. The trader, who thought it was an original line, laughed and told him that criminals' money was as good as anyone else's and that Mel should think seriously about his offer. His advisors would, of course, be compensated.

The mix of the oysters and wine on Mel's palate were exquisite, he had to admit. The trader tipped him fifty on top of his hundred-dollar fee. Mel felt good back astride his Yamahopper.

The Harleys roared up on each side of him as he rode down Second Avenue through deserted Stuyvesant Square, ceded after dark to the crack zombies. Mel and the Harleys hit a red, and he offered a courteous nod to the riders of the two big bikes. Mel felt an existential kinship with outlaws. He liked the notion of his little scooter standing shoulder to shoulder with the Harleys.

The biker on his left nodded back. The biker on his right knocked him off his scooter and unconscious with a backhanded blow from a hand wrapped in iron chain.

The biker who had hit him picked him up and put him on the pillion of the other bike, securing him to the rider with nylon rope. He put a watch cap over Mel's head, covering his mouth, and the two bikers rode off quickly. It all took less than two minutes and went unnoticed on the empty street.

Mel regained consciousness in a dark room. His head hurt. In the next room, through an open door, he could see men and women partying. He moved his arms and legs to see if he could. One of the men in the next room looked in his direction and said, "The vermin stirs."

Another man walked over to Mel and poked him in the ribs with the toe of his boot. "Know why you're here, vermin?"

"No," Mel croaked. Saying just the single word gave him a splitting headache.

"Because you made an Adder look like a dirtbag," Mel's interlocutor said. "Adders don't like that."

It was extremely difficult for Mel to follow. He was sure there was a mistake, but he didn't know what it was. The biker standing over him poked him with his boot again, harder.

"You going to make things right?" the biker inquired. "Maybe you need to think things over?" He poked him again. "Feel free to scream."

Mel's ribs now hurt almost as much as his head. That last poke may have broken something. He thought about how long it would be until he was missed. It could be days, he realized. His comings and goings were always erratic, and no one would think twice about a few days of no Mel.

He thought about why the Adders would turn on him. There were fierce debates within the international squatters' movement between the Black Rose Anarchists and the Red Rose Leninists. He was a Black Rose, and had often and vituperatively denounced the Leninists. Was there a biker-Leninist alliance of which he was unaware? It seemed far-fetched.

Then he thought about Tramp and Siobhan's boyfriend. Everything fell into place. But something was, obviously, very wrong. He wondered what the biker meant by "make things right."

He spent a couple of painful hours trying to find a comfortable position on the floor. When the biker returned, Mel said, "Okay, I'll make things right, like you say."

"How?" the biker said.

"You tell me," Mel said. "I just want to get out of here."

The biker took a piece of paper out of his pocket. He put on an incongruous pair of half-glasses in order to read. "Number one," he read from it, "is you write a personal letter to Shorty Harris, apologizing for tricking him into beating on his Nam brother." The biker took off his glasses and said, "I would make it a really good apology, if I was you. Shorty's feelings are really hurt. Turns out the guy saved his life in Nam."

He replaced the glasses and read on. "Number two is you write a letter to all your buddies on the computer thingie of yours explaining how you lied about your girlfriend and were stupid jealous, but now you see the light and want everyone to know what a great person she is and what a slimeball you are. Really make it sing, you hear what I'm telling you?"

He seemed to expect an answer. Mel contemplated the repercussions of such a letter. The biker took a step toward him and Mel said, "I hear you."

"Which brings up the question of whether you're stupid enough to change your mind once you're out of this room. What do you think about that?" The biker tapped his boot tip slowly on the floor while he waited for Mel's answer.

Mel had no idea what part of New York he was in. He was not a person who tended to think of the police as an ally. "I'm cool," he said. "You don't have to worry about me."

"You ready?" the biker said. He had a yellow pad and a pen. He threw them on the floor next to Mel. "Two letters," he said. "Beautiful letters. Write like an angel. Get going."

Chapter 29

Ukiah, Wednesday, July 10

JIMMY CORR SHOWED HIS ID TO THE DEPUTY at the front desk and said he was here to see his client, Ernest Fresser. The deputy conducted him to an interview room and told him to wait.

Jimmy looked at his notes. His client was charged with murder, armed robbery, and passing counterfeit money. It was a big uptick for the young lawyer in terms of legal responsibility. Up to now, his biggest case had been defending the civil rights of the Tonuma County School Board in Utah. The board wanted to change the school's nickname from the Rays of Purple to the Rebels, Tonuma having been originally settled by ex-Confederate soldiers. Four of the eighteen black people in the county agreed to let the ACLU sue on their behalf. The federal judge told the school board that if they were tired of being Rays of Purple, they could find a nickname that didn't stir up the past. Shelby had been disbelieving of the verdict and had acted like Jimmy had personally let down the white race.

Corr existed on generally uneasy terms with his employer. Corr's father was an apostle of Reverend Footman's, and Jimmy knew his own employment derived from the misapprehension that as his father's son, he shared his father's principles. Shelby and

Footman had interviewed him in Shelby's Pocatello office. Jimmy had lied like a rug. He needed the job.

Jimmy's current circumstances, after an undistinguished academic career at Baylor University in Waco, Texas, were that he lived rent free in his dad's house in Arcata, in return for two hours a day of morning chores—slopping the pigs, cleaning out the rabbits' hutch, and whatever else needed doing. Then he took a long hot shower, blasting the barnyard smells off his body and reminding himself that he was an officer of the court.

Jimmy had attended Baylor during a golden age, when it became the first big school in the Deep South to recruit athletic blacks. The university was rewarded with football dominion and became known as the progressive bastion of Southern Baptists. At Baylor, it had become grounds for suspension to say the N word where an administrator could hear you. Jimmy had felt proud to be part of that era.

These days, Jimmy's dad expected his son at the dinner table at six promptly, for a grace-saying that could last up to forty-five minutes and consisted of Dad wishing the worst, in considerable detail, upon his myriad enemies. The N word was prominent. Jimmy nodded along, waiting for his father to consider his foes suitably admonished, at which point food consumption could begin. Jimmy spent much of the rest of his time staring into space.

Ernie Fresser's case rekindled his spirits a bit. He looked at his pad and the notes he had made. It was all way beyond his competence, but it did not involve pigs. He would listen to Fresser's story and hope for a bad search or some other escape hatch to emerge.

The door opened, and a tall man in a suit entered. The man shook Jimmy's hand, called him Counselor, and identified himself as a special investigative agent of the US Secret Service. Cal Albright hadn't mentioned the Secret Service on the phone. Jimmy felt even more out of his depth. The agent said he wanted to give the counselor some context before Mr. Corr met with his client. They had his client on film, the agent said, both passing the bills and buying the getaway van. As for the murder charge, they had uncovered an Ingram Mac-10 in the back of a closet at Ernie's house, under a pile of Nazi propaganda.

"We were confident that this weapon was used to murder Yosh Steinmetz," the agent said. "Extremely confident. But the ballistics check came back negative, quite a surprise. Of course, we can put Mr. Fresser away for life with what we have. The murder would just put a bow on it."

The agent let Jimmy sit with the information for a long minute. Jimmy had taken notes while the agent retailed the evidence, but now he was just doodling on his pad, triangles inside of circles inside of squares inside of triangles.

"There's a silver lining here, perhaps," the agent said suddenly. "If the murder rap lands somewhere else, and if your client fully cooperates on the larger matter, he could serve a nominal sentence, and then spend the rest of his life with his wife and little girl."

"The larger matter?" Jimmy said. The agent looked at him sharply, but something about Jimmy's clueless expression seemed to soften him.

"We believe your client is a small cog in a large, seditious machine, based in Ararat, Nevada," the agent intoned. "I assumed you had some familiarity there, given whom you work for."

Jimmy didn't know anything about a big seditious machine. Shelby told Jimmy nothing more than the bare facts of any given assignment. Jimmy's father came back from his Ararat pilgrimages filled with grandiose ideas about the impending victories of the white race, but the son had ascribed his father's notions to a rich fantasy life.

"I, ah, no," Jimmy said. "I am not aware…" He got a grip and said, "You want him to cooperate, I get that. I need to talk to him."

The Secret Service agent left the room, and the deputies brought in a shackled Ernie Fresser. His eyes were bloodshot. He looked to his lawyer as if he might have been recently weeping. Fresser peered at Jimmy and said, "How old are you? You a Jew lawyer?"

"I'm twenty-six," Jimmy said, adding a year. "I am not Jewish."

"I don't trust Jews," Ernie said. Jimmy didn't say anything, which seemed to arouse Ernie's suspicions. "What about you?"

"I'm not Jewish, as I just said," Jimmy said, and then, quickly, "You got a family, don't you, Mr. Fresser? Tell me about them."

It was calculated on Jimmy's part—a way to soften Ernie to accept the bargain the Secret Service agent had proposed. He didn't expect the question to have such a devastating effect. Ernie started to babble about his daughter screaming while the officers led him out in handcuffs. Then, he couldn't continue. Tears rolled down his cheeks.

"You know, Mr. Fresser," Jimmy said. "You have a choice here. We can fight these charges, though the film is pretty damning, or we could talk to the government about a deal."

"What deal?" Ernie said.

"Well," Jimmy said. "The agent was telling me they think you might have useful information about some kind of conspiracy." Ernie blinked. "Something to do with Ararat, Nevada?"

"Not going to work for the ZOG," Ernie mumbled. Jimmy didn't hear much conviction in his voice.

"It's possible to arrange the terms of these agreements," Jimmy said. "What you'll tell them, what you won't." Jimmy didn't know if this were true at all, but figured it was worth a try. "You don't want to be separated from your family forever, do you?" Ernie grunted. "So you could offer to restrict your testimony, and see what they offer in return. Then you can decide. What can you offer them?"

Ernie was silent.

"I mean, the, uh…" Jimmy cleared his throat. "…movement against the ZOG needs its true soldiers to stay out of jail.

"And with their families," he added, driving the nail home.

He watched his client crumbling. "All right," Ernie said. "Let's see what they ask."

Chapter 30

San Francisco, Thursday, July 11

ESTEBAN, IN HIS CITROËN COFFIN IN THE BACK of the garage, and Spider, in his bed, both slept like dead men Wednesday night. Spider awoke early Thursday. It took him a minute to remember where he was and what had happened. Once he did, he went back to sleep. He had formed a plan to dispose of the body, but he needed to wait until nightfall. Eventually, he dragged himself to Belle's for breakfast and considerable coffee. Then he went to work at the shop, keeping the car in his sight.

Mikael worked late, so Spider did too. When Mikael finally shoved off at eight, Spider put a big casting pole and some lures in the backseat and attached a shop crane to the trailer hitch.

He drove across the Bay Bridge and north for ten miles to the San Pablo Point exit. He had fished from the jetty there once at night, with anchovies for leopard shark. He thought it would suit his purposes.

The jetty was broad enough for cars and a mile long. Hispanic and Asian families drove out on weekends. Stolid fathers cast long lines for kingfish, perch, smelt, flounder, sole, sharks, skates, and rays, while their families picnicked and the kids played touch football on the jetty. When the ball went in the water, one of the dads took his long net and fished it out.

At night, there were no families. The night was still young and only a few lovers' cars dotted the jetty. The end was empty in Spider's headlights. He drove out to the point and turned the Citroën around, so its trunk faced the Bay. He could see if anyone approached, and, if need be, blind them with the DS's headlamps, set iconically high on the fenders. He set up a rod holder and a canvas chair, cast his line, and spent fifteen minutes playing the role of a nocturnal shark fisherman.

The moon shone through the clouds. Spider could make out the blowing, grinning whale, which was the logo of the Del Monte Fishing Co., whose abandoned warehouse loomed on the shore. He detached the shop crane from the hitch and waited. When a cloud obliterated the moon, he took a last look around and then winched the crane to hoist the Esteban package from the trunk. He had fastened barbells to the tie-downs. He pivoted the neck of the crane and lowered it as far as it would go. It was still eight feet above the water line. There would be a splash. It couldn't be helped.

He released the jaw of the crane. The splash seemed supersonic. He resumed his ersatz pursuit of the leopard sharks. When it was apparent that he had aroused no suspicion, he reeled in his line and reattached the crane to the hitch. He thought about the strange gun he was about to jettison. He had flirted with the notion of waving the gun in Schollmeyer's face, but he saw little point to that. Let the agent pursue his Aryans. He took the metal box with the automatic weapon and lofted it out as far as he could into the deep water.

The DS squatted, waiting, like a resting big cat. Spider turned the key in the ignition, and the car boosted itself upward, powered by the hydropneumatic suspension. Spider drove back down the jetty toward the freeway. He felt pretty good, all things considered.

In the morning, he made coffee and then found his way to the garage, entering from the back and hearing Mikael in the front loudly saying, "I'll see if he's available." It was the code phrase they'd agreed upon, so Spider could take a covert look and see if he wanted to be available or not.

Whom he saw was Shorty. It was apparent that the Pariah was upset about something. Spider gimped out to meet him.

"Man, I've got to talk to someone," Shorty said as soon as he saw Spider. "Take a walk, huh?"

Mikael gave Spider a quizzical look. He had moved closer to the tire iron that they kept behind the counter. "It's fine," Spider said, loud enough for Shorty to hear. "Shorty and me go back."

He led Shorty out the door and turned right to head up to Bernal Hill but Shorty said, "Any bars up that way?" There was a plaintive sound to his voice. "I need about four drinks real bad." So Spider reversed course and headed toward Cortland, and then west toward Mission. The first bar on their right was the lesbian hangout, the VeeWoolf, so Spider tried to keep walking, to Hanrahan's a block away, but Shorty said, "This'll do," and made a hard right through the swinging doors.

The bartender was a smaller, beardless, less muscled near-replica of Shorty, with a sleeveless leather motorcycle vest, heavy tats, and miscellaneous metal accessories. "What'll it be, guys?" she said, giving Shorty an appreciative glance.

Shorty ordered a boilermaker and Spider a beer. The bartender pushed Shorty's money back at him and said, "Love the look."

Shorty gave the bartender a wan smile and pulled Spider over to a booth. "Man," he said, "I got to talk to someone I trust who isn't a Pariah, and you're the only person I know who halfway fits that."

Spider inclined his head to acknowledge the compliment.

"You've heard about Soufflange?" Shorty said. Spider hadn't.

Soufflange, Shorty said, was a suburb of Quebec where the majority faction of the Montreal-area Pariahs had just executed five minority-faction Pariahs. "My brothers killed my brothers," he said to Spider. "Man, I partied with all those dudes. Mohawk. Kong. Big Willie. Little Willie. Beaufrere. Mom. Grandmec. I rode with them."

Spider wondered what kind of biker would be nicknamed Mom. "These were your friends that were killed?" he said.

"Man, Little Willie shot Big Willie. Kong and Grandmec done the rest of them. All my friends…" He was in anguish.

"How did it happen?" Spider said.

Shorty's answer spanned three boilermakers and went into an obliterative level of detail about who had banged whose old lady and who was putting all the coke profits up his nose. The bottom line was that a business-first cohort had eliminated a hedonistic element that was considered a security risk. For Shorty, it violated a first principle: Pariahs were supposed to die for each other, not kill each other.

"How do the other Pariahs feel?" Spider said.

"It's not so personal to them. They don't know those guys. But I lived up there two, three years after Nam. I cannot believe this shit went down."

Spider didn't have much to offer. It was a new moral dilemma to him. He wondered if Shorty had made good on his promise to deal with Mel.

"Are you sure that what you heard happened in Quebec is true?" he said. "Things can get twisted."

"They're dead," Shorty said. "There's no doubt."

"Family fights are the worst," Spider said. It seemed a meaningless platitude to him, but Shorty took some comfort from it.

"I never had a family," he said. He seemed to notice his environment for the first time. The bar was adorned with blown-up photos of Barbara Stanwyck, Joan Crawford, Greta Garbo, Katharine Hepburn, and Marlene Dietrich. The bathroom doors said Hers and Hers.

"What the fuck?" Shorty said. "Where did you take me?"

"You took you," Spider pointed out. "Did you have a chance to follow up about the bad information you got?"

The question seemed to cheer Shorty up a little. "Didn't I tell you I would?" he said.

"How did it go?"

"Good," Shorty said. "Really good. Excellent. You'll see." He raised his hand, and the bartender brought them another round. Spider pushed his beer away.

"I got to be somewhere," he said. It didn't seem essential to inform Shorty it was the quarterly meeting of the Citizens' Advisory Board to the San Francisco Police Commission.

"Little Willie and Big Willie," Shorty said. "They were like twins. You couldn't tell 'em apart, except Big Willie was five-four and Little Willie was six-eight. Man, it used to crack us up, to watch people's heads snap when they got introduced."

"Be strong," Spider said, and got up to go. It seemed an odd thing to advise a Pariah, but Shorty took it to heart, lurching to his feet and enveloping Spider in a bear hug.

Chapter 31

Alamogordo, New Mexico, and San Francisco
Friday, July 12, to Saturday, July 13

BREAKFAST WITH THE ALAMOGORDO CHEMICAL WORKERS WAS A disaster. The plant's owner had instituted profit-sharing and the men had bought in completely. They had become investors, with a stake in success. Anything that drove down profits was not in their interest, including safety procedures, additional workers, and, of course, lawsuits.

"What is your health worth?" Siobhan asked them.

"I got all the kids I need," one of the men replied. "More than I need."

"Look," said another, "table salt will kill you, you take too much."

The afternoon paper brought news of a flash flood that killed eleven small children and four adults in Arizona the day before. The story played up the pathos of the bucolic swimming hole, with Mexican-American families cooling off from the desert heat, never hearing the faint warning signals of the sudden summer downpour fifteen miles upstream. Fires had cleared ridges and slopes of vegetation on land baked slick and hard by constant high temperatures, so there was nothing to slow the water. The body of the girl whose quinceañera was the occasion had been found four miles downstream.

Siobhan knew the paper was wallowing; still, it made her miss Spider. She remembered their own escape in the mountain canyon, how calm he was. There was a solid core to Spider, a kind of basic know-how. He knew how to dance with her in a Phoenix bar; he knew how to fix her Fiat; he knew how to avoid a flash flood in an Aravaipa Canyon arroyo; he knew how to make her come and how to make her laugh; he knew how to make that stupid squid dish; and he even knew, in a weird way, how to deal with her going to New York, which is to say he knew how to stay in the picture even if he never actually showed up.

It made sense, all of a moment, to pick up the motel phone and dial the number of the New People's Garage.

•••

AFTER THE "DUMP BELLE? LIKE HELL!" HAD PROJECTED Spider into the public eye, the mayor's community liaison had called, to ask him to be his district's representative on the Citizens' Advisory Board to the San Francisco Police Commission.

"Why me?" he had said to the liaison.

"We want people with no ax to grind," the liaison had answered. "Neighborhood businesspeople. Respected, ax-free, moderate people. Your neighbors think well of you."

That was more than five years ago at a time when the cops were widely perceived to be wilding. They had inducted a new cadet by forcing him to be fellated by a prostitute, while tied to a chair, in front of his fellow cadets and superiors. "Sure," Spider had told the liaison. A Commission! It sounded kind of exotic.

Nothing much changed in how the police operated, but the Commission had turned into a permanent fixture. Every three months the commissioners sat in uncomfortable high-backed chairs in the City Hall public meeting chamber and listened to citizens' complaints and the police's defensive retorts.

Today, the chief himself was testifying. He shook his white-maned Irish head and said that if you associated with people who limped, eventually you might limp yourself. He meant that cops who associated with criminals couldn't help behaving criminalish themselves.

The black lawyer from the Western Addition wanted to better understand the chief's turn of phrase. If cops who associated with criminals became bad cops, did the evil then spread through the department like mold?

The chief tossed his mane in disgust and said, "That's ridiculous."

The lawyer from the City Attorney's office said, "It's a legitimate question, Chief." She let her eyes sweep the commissioners while awaiting his reply. When her eyes met Spider's, she smiled. It wasn't the first time she had done that. She was attractive but petite, not really his type. But one could adapt. Was he single again and returning to the fray? His heart quailed at the prospect. But hanging onto Siobhan was nuts. There was, all too definitely, a pattern here.

When the meeting ended and he drove back to the shop, Mikael said Siobhan had called. On cue, the phone rang again. Mikael answered and handed the phone to Spider wordlessly.

"I miss you," Siobhan said. "I got my head cleared, and when it cleared up, there you were."

"You sure it was me?" he said.

"Pretty sure," she said. "I thought I'd come by and check."

"When would that be?" he said.

She told him she could be there the next day, Saturday, if that worked for him. He said he could probably clear his calendar.

She called back in an hour to say she could get an early flight out of Albuquerque and be at SFO at eleven. Spider called the operations manager of the Ahwahnee Hotel in Yosemite Park, who was thrilled at the prospect of a house call from the demiurge who kept his 1964 DS on the road. As it happened, they'd had a late cancellation of the Queen Elizabeth Suite, if that would meet Spider's rigorous standards?

Waiting for her Saturday morning at SFO, Spider thought about her previous arrival, less than a month ago, and all that had happened since. His groin was still a distressed zone. He could walk well enough, but when he thought about lovemaking with Siobhan, the stiffening was painful, and he decided to think about other things—like what to tell her about the Pariahs' attack and about shooting and dumping the Colombian guy. He felt reluctant to stir the bad shit that had gone down.

When she disembarked, she embraced him enthusiastically. He couldn't suppress a yelp of pain when she ground into him.

"What's wrong?" she said.

"Basketball," he croaked. "I had a close encounter with a big knee."

"Oh," she said. "Maybe I can make it better."

"Here," he said, handing her a brochure for the Ahwahnee. "I thought we'd celebrate your return in style. This room will do, I think," he said. He had circled the Queen's Suite.

Her eyes widened as she read the brochure's description of the four-poster canopied bed upon which Elizabeth II had writhed away a queenly night two years before. It was listed at a queen's ransom— two hundred dollars a night. "It's high season," she said. "And it costs a fortune."

He told her about his intimate relationship with the operations manager and that the room was to be theirs. "It has a hand-crafted bidet," Spider said. "What's a bidet?"

Siobhan clarified.

"I've got some mushrooms," Spider said. "We'll have mushrooms and room service and the queen's bidet. With a view. Let's hit the road."

In the car, he asked about her case. He would tell her about Esteban later. Or maybe never. If she wanted to talk about why she needed a break from him and why the break was now over, it was up to her. The weather in the Park was glorious. He drove up the Tioga Pass Road to the May Lake trailhead. They dropped the mushrooms and set off on the short hike. In Arizona, they had once eaten mushrooms and wandered around Aravaipa till nightfall, retracing their steps with difficulty in the chill night air. This time, they lay naked on the rocks above the lake. A hiker clomped on the trail below. "Beautiful day!" he chimed, continuing on his trek.

"Thanks for the observation," Siobhan said politely, several minutes later.

They clambered down as the sun set. Still high, Spider drove slowly back to the hotel, where they ordered room service—salmon filet and asparagus and bottles of cold mineral water. They both had terrific thirsts, and drank the water greedily.

Siobhan entered the queen's bathroom. Spider could hear the shower, and then a different running-water sound, and then Siobhan cackling, and then a flush. The sequence was repeated twice. When she came out of the bathroom, she was wearing on her head a hand towel she had tied into a crown. The hotel's thick terry white robe hung loosely on her, unbelted.

The phone rang. Spider regarded it balefully. He had only shared his whereabouts with Mikael. What couldn't wait?

"It's Shorty," the Pariah said. "Mission accomplished, old buddy. Tell your lady to go on that computer doodad of hers."

Siobhan was doing her personal version of a Michael Jackson moonwalk. The robe fell open as she moved.

"Not interrupting anything, am I?" Shorty said. He laughed lewdly. "Your mechanic didn't want to give up the number, but he agreed to make an exception for an old friend with good news."

Eight days had passed since Spider's beating; feeling had returned to his nether regions. The last thing Spider felt like doing was suggesting Siobhan open up her luggable Kaypro, but he did.

"Holy shit," Siobhan said, looking at the screen. "Mel confessed. I can't believe this is real."

Spider looked over her shoulder:

> *To the People of the Grapevine: I have really fucked up. I got in a jealous rage when Siobhan dumped me and I misused my root privileges. I sent email in her name maligning the people on the Grapevine. I am ashamed. I am resigning from the Grapevine community.*
> *With heavy heart,*
> *Mel*

Siobhan's *calamityjane* inbox overflowed with apologies. It turned out that everyone had always liked her immensely, which had made her denunciation of the Grapevine community so painful, which in turn had inspired so many venomous, wounded replies. Everyone wanted to be friends again. Siobhan was deeply touched. It struck Spider as wacko. She hadn't known these people in the first place; then they had turned on her; and now they welcomed her back to their midst. But she still didn't know them. "Enough," Siobhan said. "Stand up." He did and she shed the robe and embraced him. "How's your poor little thing?" she asked.

They were in the body-high endgame of the mushroom trip, when physical sensations are almost painfully intense. Their lovemaking had to be slow. It seemed to last forever. Spider wanted it to last forever. When they were done, they lay quietly beside each other.

"I didn't think you were coming back," Spider said.

"I wasn't sure," Siobhan said. "But I am now."

"Really?"

She got out of bed, got something out of her bag, and brought it back to Spider. "Look," she said, and handed him the familiar plastic container with the rounded top. She flicked the tab, and it opened to show the diaphragm snug inside.

"You forgot!"

"You're entitled to your opinion," she said. "This is America."

Acknowledgements

A BOOK THIRTY-FOUR YEARS IN THE MAKING GETS prodded and abetted by many along the way. In particular, my wife, Jamie Stobie, found a loving but not uncritical way to pull me through a motley variety of early drafts. My constant pal, Gene Corr, suffered through infinite variations with unceasing affection, insight, and contumely. My editor, Jay Schaefer, convinced me there could be merit here, eventually. And Michelle Dotter, a rare find of Rare Bird, got me through that last stage when I couldn't part with a word but ten thousand had to go.

I thank Michael Singsen, Mark Vermeulen, Jamie Flower, Charley Seavey—stout men of the bar who tirelessly answered my legal questions and invoked their inner novelists.

Writers are generous. The ones I hang out with, anyway. Thanks: Tamim Ansary, Michael Castleman, Ken Conner, Perry Garfinkel, Mark Nykanen, Michael Rogers.

A small army of people read and commented on my various spewings. Their attention and insights meant more to me than perhaps I conveyed at the time. I thank: Michael Arehart, Christina Dragonetti, Jim Hood, Doug Jacquier, Chris Jenkins, Robert Landheer, Ron Lichty, Wendy Miller, Danny Pelsinger, Angela Siefer, Barbara Stevenson, Debby Strauss, Edward Whitmore, Mike Yeaton.

Two writers' colonies hosted me in 1985 and 1986. I thank Blue Mountain Center (and especially Harriet Barlow) and the Djerassi Institute for taking a flyer on my abilities, way back then.

Three friends who are no longer here meant a lot to me and helped me keep at it. I miss and thank Josh Hanig, Edith Konecky, and Michael Blumlein.

I move shamelessly in this book from real events and real people—to events and people that exist only in my imagination. I did a lot of reading and, with all deviations from historical reality being my own, I want to particularly thank Kevin J. Flynn and Gary Gerhardt, authors of *The Silent Brotherhood: Inside America's Racist Underground*, which is a meticulously reported, beautifully crafted, deeply empathic account of the The Order, which was responsible for the murder of Alan Berg, the Brink's takedown and much else.

With the same caveat about reality deviations, a doff of the Stetson to the ineffable Bob Boze Bell, publisher of *True West Magazine*, whose comic art has made the last fifty years more bearable for desert inhabitants, and whose evocations of his native Kingman made my writerly heart beat fast.

Mikkel Aaland inspired me with his near pathological infatuation with the Citroën automobile, and helped me, I hope, be accurate in my depictions of that goddess.

The Whole Earth 'Lectronic Link, or WELL, was a petri dish for my ideas in the eighties, and much of what I have done since loops back to it. Thanks to all the Wellbeings, and especially Tex.

And it would be the depth of ungraciousness to not mention Wikipedia. How did people write books before? Wikipedia is surely one of the good things about being alive now.

These books were helpful and I thank the authors: *Talked to Death: The Life and Murder of Alan Berg*, by Stephen Singular; *The*

Brotherhood of Murder, by Thomas Martinez; *Humboldt: Life on America's Marijuana Frontier*, by Emily Brady; *Outlaws in Babylon: Shocking True Adventures on America's Marijuana Frontier*, by Steve Chapple; *Marijuana Grower's Handbook: Your Complete Guide for Medical and Personal Marijuana Cultivation*, by Ed Rosenthal. Thanks too, to the archives of *High Times* magazine.

And, finally, it's good to have a big brother, you know? Mine, Giora Ben-Horin, was like a father to me when I was a kid and has never left my corner. Thanks for everything, Gi.